PLANET ARALIA

Journey Among the Stars

PLANET ARALIA
Journey Among the Stars

R.L. WORTHY

LEE PUBLISHING

ISBN: 979-8-9907365-6-6

Library of Congress Control Number: 2024911178

Title: Planet Aralia: Journey Among the Stars
Author: R.L. Worthy
Publisher: R.LEE Publishing
Year: 2024
Worthy, R.L. *Planet Aralia: Journey Among the Stars*. R.LEE Publishing, 2024.

Dedication

To People With Great Imaginations

Foreword

As I reflect on my childhood, a vivid memory emerges from within the depths of my past. The moments when I would escape from the hustle and bustle of my many siblings. Into my quiet sanctuary, a secret place where I could vanish. Surrounded by tall swaying stalks towering above me, I lay hidden from the outside world. This was my magical found haven. My eyes gazed upward into a captivating vast universe behind fluffy white and gray clouds.

I would spend hours watching the clouds as they morphed into various imaginary figures, forming playful faces that would fill me with wonder. Visions of simple yet mesmerizing occurrences gave hope. I was astonished and left with a sparking cascade of thoughts within my young mind. Each time I stared beyond the clouds, my imagination soared in my thoughts while I contemplated the existence of a universe beyond our own.

I realized that life must hold so much more than what I currently know. It was a moment within this space, amid the rustling stalks and the boundless sky, that my inner world flourished. My musings ventured into realms of science fiction, by my envisioned distant planets with futuristic technologies and extraordinary adventures. As I share my memories and delve into the universe,

I invite you, dear reader, to join me on a captivating journey. Allow the tales that soon follow to transport you to uncharted territories with no limits to the imagination that surpassed astronomical wonders. Embrace the excitement, mystery, and endless possibilities that await within these pages.

So, take my hand, and together, let us embark on an enthralling voyage into the realms of science fiction. May these stories ignite the same sense of awe and curiosity that once sparked within me, a child lost in a world of high stalks and boundless skies. Enjoy the adventure that lies ahead!

Table of Contents

Introduction

In the vast expanse of the universe, where the forces of good and evil collide, there exists a power greater than any other. It is a power that holds the key to solutions for every evil that threatens the realm of good.

Good and evil are intertwined, forever locked in a cosmic dance across the universe.

Beyond the reach of our sight, stars silently undergo mysterious evolution, guarding ancient secrets while veiling the birth of new worlds. Within the depths of these stars, intense heat works magic, transforming colossal crystals into liquid, birthing planetary spheres concealed within.

Stars explode and give rise to new stars, unleashing dazzling rays of light, illuminating the Milky Way and beyond.

Our universe is a realm of countless enigmas that significantly surpass the limits of human imagination, extending beyond galaxies and traversing the planets of the solar system.

There is a spectacular tale of survival in the boundless void of outer space, where enormous powers converge and generate immense energy that pulsates through space. The universe expands, accelerates, and widens its bandwidth quickly, transmitting signals to uncharted territories and revealing breathtaking splendor.

In the vastness of space, energy courses through the cosmos, similar to the pulsations of a living heart, which give birth to celestial cells.

Foreign life flourishes and evolves throughout the universe as wondrous planets come into being. Planets, known as Old-World planets, are inhabited by alien lifeforms and blessed with extraordinary symmetry, of incredible abilities, and the power to manipulate the very fabric of thought.

This is the story of a select group of aliens chosen by the universe itself to safeguard the existence of alien life. The importance of their role becomes increasingly apparent as their mystical powers, derived from the forces of the universe, unfold.

The allure of these magnificent planets grows stronger, attracting beings from corners of the universe toward their captivating galaxies.

Born with innate genius, the leaders among these aliens embark on a momentous endeavor: the creation of a vital weapon to protect their planets. This weapon, known as the Realms, is a living, operational machine that forms the backbone of the defense system of these planets. Without the Realms, these Old-World planets would be vulnerable to a multitude of dangers.

The Realms mechanics are responsible for expanding and connecting all the Old-World planets.
During the cycle of the Realms, echoes from supernatural tunes sound out among the heavens. More significant than any harmonious symphony, as the shadowy echoes reverberate throughout the universe.

The Realms serve as the crucial link between hidden planets and the wider universe, facilitating travel for the warriors who safeguard their planets.

These resolute gateways beckon travelers to pass over the vast cosmic expanse, intrigued to integrate with the aliens of these ancient celestials situated far beyond the galaxy.

Mystical portals stand as the threshold between universes and the enigmatic time-worn worlds and inhibit all who dare to embark upon the journey back or to another dimension.

As you immerse yourself in this saga, you will come to understand the profound significance of the Realms to the alien races in certain seasons.

Prepare to be captivated by the lives of extraordinary aliens, particularly those on planet Aralia. Amid the awe-inspiring beauty of the universe, there lies a deeper story waiting to be unraveled by the tale of Great and Elder Kings, warriors, and their enigmatic leaders.

As you delve deeper into this narrative, you will grasp the importance, crucial growth, and knowledge aimed at the young generations, who regard the legends of old and their great kingdoms as mere myths.

Soon, they will discover the brilliance and wisdom that their ancestors are not fables but a tangible connection waiting to awaken within them.

Among the characters that will guide us through this journey are: Tepa, daughter of the ruler of all the Old-World planets. Tepa finds joy in the tales her grandfather reads to her. Tales that fill her imagination and enchantment. Tepa feels pressure from many eyes on her and still has no idea why.

Eaton, dignitary, son of rulers. The story unfolds with the duality of his identity, son of rulers and bearer of universe-altering gifts. Self-discovery, destiny, and the balance between power and responsibility are central to his journey as he navigates a world where the fate of galaxies rests in the hands of a seemingly ordinary, leading figure with extraordinary potential.

Aether, Ancestry knowledge, leader of warriors. This enigmatic helper possesses unparalleled skills in both combat and strategy honed over centuries of existence. His commitment to all missions is unwavering, while his moves pivot along the treacherous path with a blend of grace and sheath, ensuring that the dangers lurking in the shadows remain oblivious to his presence.

Each possesses extraordinary gifts yet remain oblivious to the true extent of their potential, which will be unveiled through the revelations of the hidden ancestral tale that has long eluded the new generation.

Prepare to be drawn into a tale that transcends the boundaries of the known universe, where the fate of ancient worlds and the awakening of dormant powers intertwine.

Chapter One

KINGS CONTROL OF THE UNIVERSE

In the vast expanse of the universe, a realm of stillness and breathtaking beauty stretched as far as the eye can see, extending into infinite space. The backdrop for a tale that explored secrets of hidden celestial worlds and galaxies, where alien life thrived and celebrations abound.

The millennium passed into a period of celestial peacefulness, sanctioning Great Kings to emerge throughout the universe. They infused the galaxies with enchanting light and banished encroaching primitive darkness.

One Great King, King Odonias, was not like the other Great Kings. He was powerful, and his face gave off a strong, hypnotizing light that illuminated variations of colors. He wore full-scale armor with a mask that blended in with his face and body.

He spoke with a voice of thunder to the other Great Alien Kings. "Time is moving fast, so let us start the competitions." Although there was certainly no competition with his participation since they all saw his great abilities, they had no doubt that he was more advanced than all kings, and he gave them something to reach for.

The competitions began, creating the most out-of- mind artistry ever seen, as they began to mark the infinite universe with their fingers, creating magnificent ancestral designs and magical drawings throughout space.

These wise rulers left their mark in the competition, in the cosmos, adorning space with magnificent drawings to endure for all eternity, sealed by the stars, and will last forever.

The Great Kings' era have ended, remaining in this universe.

They were chosen because of a greater need to transcend different universal dimensions. Succeeding in each task given and proving worthiness was honored within the one who held secrets of power.

The Great Kings were tasked to leave the twelve Elder Kings to continue their work as a council in the present universe. These twelve Elder Kings were intelligent and undeniably influential. Yet, they could never possess or be as formidable with inspiring might as their predecessors retain.

Understanding the dilemma of extraordinary gifts that the Elder Kings were not blessed with prompted the Great Alien Kings to search for a gifted king to give authority over the Elder Kings. One of the Great Kings spoke boldly, "There is one known by us all, located close to this universe with power and goodness. No one is greater than King Odonias's son. The young King Odonias should succeed his father."

Young King Odonias looked at his father, with eyes piercing through, giving a look of wonder and amazement, and asked, "Why did you choose me as your successor?" The young, humble king stood, gesturing at his father, the king. Although he was elevated, his father had a power like no other, which was only felt by the young king.

The young king looked at his father with his brazen face and hypnotizing eyes and gave total attention to the Great King Odonias as he expressed his confidence in his son. "It is your destiny. This is why your gifts of exceptional and incomparable abilities are more powerful and majestic than the respected Elder Kings."

Young King Odonias, feeling a little nervous, motioned for the Great King to sit by him and carefully said to his father, "Suppose it is too soon?" The king smiled while responding to his wise son. "Remember, time is in control of your very being and destiny. It cannot be too soon."

He let the king, his father, know that he would do as he has been asked, saying, "I will remember your words and do everything to assume the task after you and the other Great Kings, who will ascent to the new dimension." Young King Odonias became an integral figure among the twelve Elder Kings.

Many across the galaxies were amazed at how the new Great King had gained admiration from numerous alien sovereigns. He was from a unique dimension in the cosmos, and he dominated with extraordinary talents distinct from the Elder Kings of profound intellectual competence.

King Odonias was a pleasure to look upon, had a greater stature than the other aliens, and his strong physique and attractiveness gave him an advantage.

He demonstrated enthused confidence, leaving an admirable impression. When he arrived in the presence of others and after he exited, a positive charge was left in the atmosphere.

However, much refusal was made to his ascent to higher ranks, which had caused jealousy to be harbored in the Elder Kings' hearts. One of the distraught Elder Kings spoke out to the others, expressing his disapproval.

Saying; "The decree given to the Elder Kings, from the Great Kings is forged, allowing the young ruler authorization to command respect if needed." And continued to say, "We the Elder Kings are responsible for the protection of respective planets and vigilantly uphold the natural order of life across their domains now feel threatened by the decision of King Odonias's authority."

Young King Odonias had long been a catalyst for ongoing peace among the Elder Kings. Recently, he had detected voices of murmurs, discontent, and brewing conflicts in their hardened hearts.

He connected to his father, within a mental state, saying, "Something is wrong here. I am sensing great turbulence, filled with unsettling emotions, jealousy, and hurt from the Elder Kings' thoughts, and they are worse than expected."

The young King Odonias said, "I never felt this feeling of hate before, and my gift of persuasion to mend their discordant hearts is not clear. It must be trickery in their minds to camouflage their thoughts."

Years passed and moved quickly, so much so that King Odonias explained to all of the aliens, "Remember the ways of the universe. When time travels at a fast pace, it means the universe is making room for something to take place."

The young king continued to safeguard his dimension in the universe, using his persuasive magic upon countless aliens to ensure peace and restrain malevolent forces from unleashing calamities.

King Odonias returned to his home; a mysterious, secluded, hidden realm concealed from the interference of other aliens unless one is invited. Some speculated his origin was located in a large span of dimension outside their ability to begin to comprehend, which creates another myth that adds to the mystique surrounding him.

Although the Elder Kings were aware of King Odonias's home world, listening to tales for centuries led to anxiety among them from not knowing.

For years, anticipating the return of the Great King, yearning for the opportunity to explore his enigmatic realm and share in its knowledge and prosperity, never happened.
This caused an emotion that left the Elder Kings with a feeling of unworthiness in their heart.

Young King Odonias moved on to complete other tasks enthusiastically searching the universe for a mate. He found a beautiful princess in his mother's world. His mother, a mighty queen, always knew who he would mate with. It could only be an alien princess from his mother's world. A princess with honor and strength from a tribe of mighty power who could safeguard the young king and has all the requirements to take care of the task given to him by the universe.

King Odonias's wife materialized, bearing a glow around her, a powerful aura that enhanced the mysteries of the greatest of kings. King Odonias was instantly attracted to the princess when he was introduced by his mother.

His mother was a queen of a magnetic universe, and his father lived with her when he could. His mother's duties far exceeded King Odonias's duties. The queen naturally carried an impressive force around her, which armed her with the skill to fulfill her appointed responsibilities.

When the young king met the princess, he tried to win her heart by using his power of persuasion, the gift he used to keep peace among the kings and others. The beautiful young princess, realizing what he was going to try and do, brought disappointment to her. The young king's attempts to persuade her through intellect initiated her instinct. She expected more from the young king and was offended at this feeble attempt to persuade her.

His plan was to get information quickly without communicating with her. Upon obtaining knowledge from her thoughts, he believed that she would be impressed. The young king was wrong. He knew nothing about the dimension she was from, a universe no one had ever seen or accidentally visited. Which added to his curiosity and gave him more of a motive to search her thoughts. But not knowing the princess very well and having no idea who she was, maybe he had the wrong idea.

King Odonias's mother was the only one who knew the princess and how incredibly special she was. The princess was sent to the queen to live in her universe. Her kingdom sent her to learn about another universe and to experience and find her mate.

It just was not a smart thing for the young king to do, using his gift of persuasion. The princess's eyes turned a beautiful color, and a mighty aura turned into power and flowed from her eyes as she looked at him.

He said, "Wait, it is not what you think, wait."

She used her power to send the young king hurdling through space. She did not intend to hurt him because she already knew she was in love. Although she was the only one who could retrieve him from space, she did it with a smile, and at that moment, they both realized they were indeed destined for one another.

Enamored by her immunity to his persuasion, he ultimately chose her as a spiritual partner. Now, the new queen could not go back to her universe. She married knowing that King Odonias was responsible for creating a place in the universe of another dimension, and they ventured into the galaxy.

The Elder Kings began to prepare for the Season of the Stars celebration, a magnificent event, for many reasons. It was time for King Odonias to make his presence among the Elder Kings again, for the upcoming celebration. He made all the preparations needed for travel, inviting only fellow aliens sharing the genes chosen by the angels and those with a keen understanding of them.

The king's wife did not travel with him. She was waiting to give birth, nesting, and preparing for their descendant. The young queen patiently waited for King Odonias to return even before he left.

King Odonias instantly vanished from his queen's side, traversed through space, and emerged in a different dimension within the universe of the Elder Kings. The arrival of the young king was impressive and beyond mere words.
A star emerged, catching the attention of the Elder Kings.
They witnessed a rift forming in the fabric of the universe, through which the young king, Odonias, stepped out from his own realm. With great curiosity, the kings watched and briefly saw the lavish magnificence that awaited King Odonias in his hidden world.

The Elder Kings showed faces of ambiguous frowns and shook their head after witnessing the amount of emerald and gold seen in the moment of the opening to his universe. "How can someone so young have so much and never share?" With increased jealousy of King Odonias, his perceived privilege yielded more dislike throughout the years.

However, the real problem was the impact of King

Odonias and his gift of persuasion. They sought to stop him from controlling all aliens' thoughts. The twelve Elder Kings began to seek ways to create distance between themselves immediately from King Odonias. But before they could focus on King Odonias, they had a special vote among the Elder Kings to make critical changes to the realm.

Ten of the Elder Kings planned to oppose establishing Realms by voting to allow aliens unrestricted travel beyond galaxies. One out of twelve kings voted for the proposal when the votes were counted. Surprisingly, eleven kings who had initially agreed before the vote now opposed it. The end result of the vote brought turmoil among them.

Believing their thoughts or actions should remain inviolable. The crucial event fostered jealousy and growing animosity toward King Odonias more than ever, making his situation clearer as to why the kings became separated from him. After all, he held influence over all the decisions made by the Elder Kings.

Most of the king's discussions turned into something never

expected by all the Elder Kings. King Odonias explained, "Why do you lack the wisdom to see the larger picture here? The security of the universe is in jeopardy. We have to keep the Realms for the protection of the planets."

The Elder Kings, changing moods and showing an ugly, unruly nature, decided they would remove King Odonias to prevent him from using the power of his persuasion. All the Elder Kings pondered, thinking, "How do we remove him? What about the Great Kings and King Odonias from hearing the plot of his capture in our thoughts?"

Never thinking about why the young king had been given such a power of control in the first place; to control the Elder King's desires and thoughts would become the downfall of their existence. "We have to decide before the Season of the Stars celebration and before King Odonias travels back to his home, where he is protected."

Some of the Elder Kings already had a plan to destroy the young king. They just needed to get agreements from the others to move forward. This decision would cause a ripple in the universe that would never be forgotten.

Weeks before the Season of the Stars celebration, the kings sent out sources to inquire about the perfect way to remove the young king. While looking for answers and trying to find help, a message was sent privately from an unknown group. The kings found out who sent the private note. Looking uneasy and perplexed, he said with a strong, certain acknowledgment, "This note is from evil aliens from the dark hole in the universe."

"This is not a good sign. What are we truly trying to do to King Odonias? We need to think about the actions we are taking against him and the Great Kings." In an uproar, the other kings begin to question the jealousy of the Elder King, who had always wanted to take over. They did not know it was too late because two Elder Kings had already planned a meeting.

The aliens approached, offering assistance, but several Elder Kings were still skeptical. Expressing their reservations and having heard rumors about the malevolence of these dark aliens. Recognizing the potential risks, the Elder Kings became reluctant about the evil aliens' involvement. They actively sought alternative plans to not involve them.

The evil aliens had no intention of losing this opportunity. Lurking within the dark hole of space, they cunningly feigned concern for the Elder King's grievances toward King Odonias. They could not hide their evilness, for it was exposed to them by their distorted physical figures. As they spoke, sounds of reverberations came through their voices.

"Kings, we can assure you the objective is not to kill the young ruler but to remove him from power." While claiming to understand the Elder Kings' desire for freedom from King Odonias's influence, they promised a harmonious outcome for everyone involved. Under the spell of thinking and disregarded the potential consequences of their decisions.

As the Season of the Stars celebration ended, and before King Odonias returned to his protected realm, he overheard the whispers of betrayal emanating from the hearts of the Elder Kings.

King Odonias was able to filter through the camouflage, and before he could delve into their thoughts, a bag was swiftly pulled over his head, leaving him blind and vulnerable to the aliens surrounding him.

He could not see or fight the aliens that bound him. In that same moment of helplessness, he sent his thoughts to his wife, hoping she would hear and understand.

Realizing what had taken place and understanding the gravity of the situation, King Odonias's wife moved swiftly but remembered her safest course of action was to seek refuge with King Odonias's father, the Great King.

Summoning inner strength, the young queen was aware of her role and King Odonias's role. His destiny and purpose. So, she took the necessary actions she had to undertake. Without certainty, she believed one day she would have her king back.

The young queen had regrets for not attending the Season of the Stars celebration. However, King Odonias could not agree with putting their child's wellbeing at risk. The queen, missing her king, told his tribes, "It was proven to be the right decision. The result of our family being there would have been a greater mistake."

She remembered the tragic loss of her brother, which reinforced her resolve to protect their family from the clutches of the evil aliens and remove any opportunity to take someone else from the hidden universe.

Swiftly, the evil aliens transported King Odonias through the dark hole, celebrating their newfound freedom after being held captive by both King Odonias and his father, the Great King. The Elder Kings remained oblivious to the full extent of what King Odonias had been guarding.

The actions of the kings allowed evil to take King Odonias and caused the release of a manifestation of evil worse than the present. Unbeknownst to the Elder Kings, their actions allowed evil aliens to inadvertently release a dark, malevolent power, which had been trapped and abandoned between dimensions for years and was locked deep into the abyss.

The malevolent force had roamed the universe for millions of years before the Great Kings entered the first dimension of the universe. Imagine the fear they would have faced with a figure twisted and contorted, features marred by the influence of darkness. Its skin was pallid and sickly, with deep, jagged scars

Snaking across the face and body, serving as reminders of past encounters with malevolent forces. Its eyes sunken and devoid of warmth, glowing with an eerie, otherworldly light. With limbs unnaturally elongated, giving a grotesque and unsettling appearance. Emanating an aura of malevolence and corruption, their physical form was warped by the evil that had consumed them.

It took a vast number of colossal angels to defeat it and remove it from spreading evil throughout the universe, and now it was being released because of the Elder Kings.

The Elder Kings, focused on the coincidences caused by evil around them but were still out of touch with how terrible things really were. They had also forgotten about King Trios, who hailed them during their plot to remove King Odonias.

He was in distress from seeing him again, and he realized they knew nothing about him, which was not good. They did not listen to the conversation King Trios had shared with them about his travels with the Great Kings. He came to honor King Odonias but encountered the Elder Kings first. He looked forward to meeting with the young king during the Season of the Stars.

However, now, while dealing with the evil aliens, the Elder Kings had to face and deal with the king they overlooked. The Elder Kings were reserved. Knowing what they were going to do to King Odonias affected their judgment. They were cold and very rude to the Elite King, and they never logically obtained who the king was, nor did they know his reasoning or power.

The Elder King's reminiscence on the day the king entered into the universe forcefully to show his power, hailing a whistling sound with missile speed from a distant planet outside the universe.

Elite King Trios made an introduction to the Elder Kings. Saying to them, with a smile full of confidence and warmth, "I entered your universe with ten tribal communities to integrate with the inhabitants living on planet Araila. A planet the Great Kings admired.

"And told the tribes about King Odonias, who is admired and trusted." He said, "Since settling and leading the communities, I have time to talk about joining you."

The Elite King equated the knowledge from his huge universe

to this small universe and offered profound knowledge to the Elder Kings, only to become extremely disappointed in them. He said to the alien kings, "You dare treat me like I am lower than you." He became so angry he left them in haste.

While sharing with the communities about what took place with the Elder Kings caused concern for the tribe leaders. Watching how King Trios reacted with disgust, they saw something different in him; he was moving brutally, and his body started to pulsate as if it were about to burst. He explained, "They insulted me by disapproving, shunning, with laughter. I dare them."

The Elder Kings talked among themselves about the Elite King. However, because they were so vigorously immersed in the capture of King Odonias, unwariness isolated them. The Elder Kings could see he had extraordinary gifts and said, "There will not be room for this king." They said to each other again, "We have no knowledge or information about him."

King Trios's eyes were on fire. He said, "Their ignorance will bring destruction to this universe." The king's countenance changed to anger, causing him to become vulnerable. King Trios opened himself to become entangled in a terrible deed that would haunt him forever and would eventually lead him to be called the evil king.

The power King Trios carried was unrecognizable. He went to face the Elder Kings again after missing the Season of the Stars celebration. He felt something was wrong, very wrong, because he had not met King Odonias. The kings said, "You just missed your admirer a couple of days ago.
"So, tell us what makes you an Elite King, and what tricks have he brought into this universe?"

The ignorant Elder Kings were still in denial and self-absorbed about what they felt they had accomplished.
They never noticed that the Elite King Trios was quiet, for he heard the queen's and Great King's pain at the capture
of King Odonias.

Suddenly, before another word could be said, a heavy blanket of dark smoke traveled in and covered everyone in the presence of the Elite King Trios. Inside the darkness, a voice, revealing, painful sounds of echoing voices inside, almost hypnotizing to those that were listening.

The darkness said, "King Trios, join me, and I will ease your pain by giving these ungrateful kings to you."

The king asked, with concern, "What and who are you"? A voice carrying many unknown evils vibrated and spoke, "I am a power older than this universe, banished from my throne and sent out from the greatest dimension."

King Trios said, "You cannot help me because the revenge in my heart is overwhelming."

The darkness spoke again, saying, "The power of goodness is required for me to return, and if you join me, we can become greater than all entities."

The darkness could feel King Trios's anger, and he felt his anger weakening him. Slowly, the darkness began to release power to the king, and before he could resist, the king felt himself receiving strength from the mysterious dark force. The force that was hidden within the dark dimensions of an unbelievably bad place. One fateful encounter with this powerful dark spirit transformed King Trios into a dark and malevolent ghost.

Now, with the capture and absence of King Odonias, the

universe became susceptible to the same darkness; an insidious evil that emerged from the depths of the dark hole thousands of years ago was released again. This newfound evil, to most, was more menacing than the malevolent aliens themselves. It thrived on chaos and sought to capture the souls of the righteous.

The evil presence spread throughout the universe, casting a shroud of sadness upon a once harmonious cosmos. The darkness began to infiltrate the hearts of the kings, giving rise to jealousy and kindling the flame of malevolence in those susceptible to its influence.

Now, the same evil was finally able to enter the universe, for there was no one to keep it trapped. Its only purpose was to capture the souls of good. Signs of evil darkness moved throughout the universe, and complete sadness followed the Elder Kings. In the beginning, the entrance of the dark force got its power from the kings' agreement to allow the evil aliens to capture King Odonias.

Darkness fell throughout the universe. There was confusion among them, and suddenly, without any indication, change came immediately. True hate was born. The darkness brought forth a change to the Elder Kings, who carried jealousy within their hearts and caused a spirit of evilness to produce itself in those who were weak.

The evil aliens who received power from the dark spirit imprisoned the kings, who opened their hearts to it. The aliens and alien kings who found their strength from love were able to block the spirit of evil and received the power to conquer from angels. There is a power greater than all power, and there is an answer for every evil that comes against good. Where evil lies, you will always find good, wherever it appears, in the universe.

The actions of the Elder Kings gave way to evil, who, in return, captured them and their planets, never being seen again. To prevent further havoc from the pair, and before losing control of the universe, angels sent warriors to banish King Trios, who became an evil ghost, into a forbidden black hole, ensuring the alien posed no more threats.

After the safe containment of the malevolent entity, the angels left again from the Old-World planets. The universe was left with two powerful sides. A side that represented profound immorality, wickedness, and supernatural force, which stalked the universe with its relentless evil.

On the other side were spiritual forces and great warriors sent by angels. The warriors were vital to the livelihood of all the planets in the universe, as well as those hidden by distance. The warriors had been protecting Old-World planets for ages. They were sent to rule and combat evil until evil diminished. With the strength of the warriors, the evil aliens were pushed back into the dark hole.

They were habitually reappearing to find a way onto the protected planets. They never succeeded because the warriors were always waiting on them, and battles arose. The Season of the Stars was an exciting time of celebration for the angels and warriors in the heavens.

The evil aliens chose to continually dismantle the Season of the Stars celebration in hopes of breaking the spiritual connection and intimidating the warriors. They were in a trance, with only thoughts of war beyond the realms of the universe, until the hour of intrusion of the Realms to the planets. Until then, they would continue to cause multiple battles with massive disturbances, loud thunder, lightning, and outbursts of storms, which kept the battles hidden from being noticed by the inhabitants of the Old-World planets.

When storms, rain, and thunder come, planet inhabitants take cover to protect their homes, not knowing a battle is taking place. The inhabitants of the planets had been protected by the warriors for a span of time. They would have to learn quickly about many things they had never experienced before. Changes that were about to take place on their planets.

Chapter Two

PLANET ARALIA

Beautiful Aralia, positioned within the glistering Milky Way among smaller planets. It was an intoxicating planet.

It was said you could feel the warmth from its gleaming beacon, which was so bright it attracted those in the galaxy that would bring harm to the planet and its inhabitants.

For thousands of years, warriors functioned as guardians, standing vigilant, warding off any malicious aliens that attempted to harm Aralia and spread evil across the universe.

The warriors had unwavering dedication that ensured Aralia remained a sanctuary of peace and goodness amid the cosmos. Warriors lived on top of the highest mountains on the planet in tall buildings built with materials that had lasted millions of years. The height of the building flowed into the Realms so they could tower into the universe from Aralia and other planets.

Thousands of years ago, after the wars, Aralia, a striving planet, was invaded by evil, along with other planets in the galaxy. No one traveled to these planets because darkness fell upon them, changing the Old-World planets to become full of hate and death.

Galaxies stayed this way until warriors, who battled for good, defeated the evil raiders and took control of the lost planets, which are the Old-World planets, remembering how beautiful the Old-World planets once were. How they were once known all over the universe. Aralia was one of those unforgettable planets.

Many years ago, evil aliens set out to invade the universe, leaving abandoned planets behind their pathway and capturing the most gifted leaders to control the aliens from their planets. Warrior fighters reigned throughout the galaxies, discovering destruction caused by the evil aliens. They made an agreement to keep control of all the evil aliens, understanding the importance of banding as one team to conquer them.

As years passed, battles were won, and the warrior's planets were protected. Every season, the warriors successfully hindered the evil aliens, banishing them into a distant universe's black hole. Following each victorious season, the warriors would retreat to their home planets by passing through the Realms. Among these planets was Aralia, where they found solace and rest after their strenuous battles against the wicked aliens.

There was periods when evil aliens faced defeat, they cunningly concealed themselves amid the comets and asteroids within the solar system. Positioned within hidden vantage points, they were persistent in creating evil tactics aimed at diverting the attention of the valiant warriors.

They were a present threat to the warriors by camouflaging themselves, bringing destruction and ruin to both the universe and the Old-World planets. The battles could never stop until evil aliens were subdued. Saving Old-World planets was important to all planets in the universe. If a battle was ever lost to the evil aliens, there would be great travail in the galaxy.

Aralia would be the next planet for evil aliens to attack.

After the total purging of the evil aliens from the planets in the Old World, a change took place in the atmosphere, which caused a glacial transformation on Aralia. Mysterious gemstones rained on the land like rainfall. These beautiful gemstones were throughout the mountains and valleys. The mountain peaks were so high that the planet reflected beautiful colors from the gems, creating a constant flash of colors seen in the universe.

Imagine walking the streets of this beautiful planet. With every step, you see breathtaking sights, revealing the warmth of something unique and special all around, and underneath your feet, you get a glimpse of gems entrenched into the streets.

The benefit from the richness and planet life formed Aralia for the life of other exceptional features, the communities of extraordinary tribal aliens. Aliens that, over the years, had survived life threatening situations, leaving magnificent results from thousands of years ago. They had advanced to nurture spirituality, strength, and morality throughout the tribal tribes. The warriors, not known by the new generation, were for a purpose.

In fact, the new generation had no idea about the strength and gifts of their ancestors, but time and destiny would take over, and all would be made known very soon.

Chapter Three

TEPA

Tepa adored her life and found joy in the tales told by her grandfather. Tales that filled her imagination and enchanted her.

She remembered him saying to her as a young girl, discovering the castle before the visitors arrived, "Tepa, have you ever wondered why the walls in this castle feel so alive?" His eyes glowed with hidden wisdom.

Tepa, the young and inquisitive girl, looked up from her amusement with a curious expression. "Alive! Grandpa, walls are just walls." He chuckled with a deep, resonant voice. "No, my dear, these walls hold the tales of our ancestors. Touch and feel them. You might just catch a glimpse of the past."

Her eyes widened, and she slowly approached the cold corridor wall. She hesitated for a moment before reaching out.

As her fingers grazed the surface, the chill transformed into a comforting warmth, and the wall lit up with ethereal glows. He said to her, "Look closely." He gave her a look of acceptance, which encouraged her.

Images and illusions danced before her eyes. Tribal sketches, alien landscapes, and stories were etched in the fabric of the castle. Tepa lingered and gazed, feeling a connection to something larger than herself.

"Grandfather, the walls are holding and showing the same stories you have read to me," she said with a sense of wonder in her voice.

He nodded. With pride, his eyes filled with proudness as he realized she did remember the stories he read to her. He said, "These are tales of our legendary ancestors, warriors, and leaders who paved the way for our existence."

Tepa's innocent demeanor gave out a spark of realization for her. She quietly said, "Grandfather, I feel like a part of the wall. Is there something else you have to tell me?" Looking at him for answers, saying, please tell me, with her eyes. Her grandfather smiled, saying, "One day, the walls will reveal your path, and you will lead your generation. For you are the bridge between the old and new worlds, destined for greatness."

Tepa absorbed his words and explained, saying, "I feel a heavy weight from my lineage, with expectations upon my shoulders, and yet no idea of my destiny."

Grandfather spoke quietly over her, saying, "Give peace to her eager mind that can't be challenged at this moment until she learns of the hidden mysteries that await her.

"Believe the castle and its living walls, which have become a silent witness to your unfolding destiny and true identity amid the secrets of your descendants."

Although Tepa was incredibly young, this special time together with her grandfather created a special bond between them. As years passed, she pondered, "Why do my parents have to travel so much? and leave me in the hands of others?

They will never see who I have already become." Tepa's parents traveled the Aralia planet and governed most of the universe. Tepa's mother told her,

"Remember how Nan, your governess, told you that she will always love and protect you? It is important for you to learn to depend on yourself and trust your actions. So, I believe you will trust the members of your community who will give their lives to safeguard you."

Tepa's mother continued to listen and watch her with concern, saying to her daughter, "You are a very humble and agreeable daughter. One day, there will be a time when you have to be brave and very strong."

Tepa realized that her innocence gleamed as a false beacon. "I am very strong and aware, and nothing can surprise me, so, my innocence will continue to be a beacon, and no one will really know what I am capable of." She smiled suggestively but kept a deep awareness of the deeper significance of who she needed to become from the attention she received.

Tepa's father was listening to the conversations and expressed to her mother, "Beyond Tepa's youthful exterior, she is obviously observant and values obedience, patience, and goodness, which is the key to power, which is everything she needs to reach her destiny."

Tepa listened intently and responded quickly, "The moment the door to my purpose in life opens, I will be ready."

Tepa and many like her were considered the new generation. She was the granddaughter of the highest greatest in the universe, with boundless influence next to her father, who was a leader of all universal planets.

She lived in a world of considerable expectations of success, which generated a healthy atmosphere to create space for natural curiosity. With many secrets around her and, no knowledge of what these secrets were, made Tepa anxious. Knowing that they existed in connection of her identity, to the elders of the past. There is an expectation from those who advised and trained her to become a leader and to understand the path of her ancestors.

Tepa adored her life and talked about her amazing grandfather to anyone who would listen, expressing and saying, "While I listen to the tales told by my grandfather, it fills me with joy." She also thought about the images that were embedded in her experiences during these special times. She smiled and showed her unique, attractive features. Thinking to herself, she said aloud, "These tales have come alive and filled my imagination. I love the enchantment."

Her innocence shone, and she was fully aware that there was a deeper significance in the attention she received. She anticipated the outcome of a moment that would greatly open the door to her purpose in life.

Her parents continued their travels as they governed galaxies of universal planets while leaving trusted members of the community to safeguard her.

Tepa loved living in a magnificent castle developed by ancestors thousands of years ago. Throughout the castle were countless rooms and corridors. Tepa talked about how the castle was magic, saying, "One moment, I touch the wall, and it feels cold, and in the spit of a second, the walls immediately turn warm."

The touch on the wall lit up and glowed, showing hidden illusions of a beautiful life that looks extremely real. Throughout the corridors of the castle, there were magnificent carvings symbolizing the universe, with tribal alien sketches on mountain ranges and other designs displayed. The longer someone looked at the wall, the more they saw stories unveiling before their eyes. Tepa always believed these were signs of the ancestors.

Tepa's favorite place in the castle was the library. She enjoyed walking through the library. In the artifacts room, there were structures holding individual body frames along the wall. They were preserved in super thin wax and made alien bodies look genuinely alive. Tepa attempted to remain calm, though she struggled until she left the hallway.

Each visit to the artifacts room felt weird and very uncomfortable with the mysterious surroundings of preserved bodies. Although she felt a sense of pride in imagining her ancestors as extraordinary beings, she could not shake off the unease that filled the air.

Tepa proudly imagined the history of her ancestors as great aliens. This information was from the many declarations in the history of the ancestors for the new generation. In order for anyone to find their place in the universe, they had to know where they came from.

Aralia stood as a profound symbol of ancient wisdom and intelligence. Upon arrival, guests were warmly greeted by Tepa's father, a distinguished leader overseeing universal peace within an intelligence agency for various planets. To make sure the knowledge flowed in the community, guests were graciously permitted to access the distinguished library in the castle.

Visitors flocked to delve into the study of their earliest historical artifacts, tracing the planet's evolution and the passage of generations. The library was abundantly stocked, with collections of books spanning centuries containing a wealth of philosophical insights.

It was an extremely functional place in the castle and got great attention from everyone who entered. The halls were long and wide. The entrance faced a magnificent wall of carved writing of words moving mysteriously. The wall had become a discussion area for guests, and after experiencing it, there were many inspiring and profound thoughts about their identity and purpose.

The guests, captivated by the powerful and mesmerizing imagery seen, were evoked by the words shown, and after seeing the wall for the first time, they were eager to share how the words generated an enchantment of feelings and prompted a spiritual awakening in each of them in unusual ways. Some had described how they felt hypnotized, and it tried to pull them into it.

These words kept the community in the same thought pattern, and they believed in the importance of the message and understood the power behind the meaning of the words. The words were designed and sculpted by ancient architects. The words written on the wall encouraged goodness. It stated: "Goodness is in the midst of power."

Chapter Four

THE LIBRARY: HIDDEN SECRETS

Tepa spent most days and nights in the library, listening to the stories told by community leaders and others who were from faraway places. The technology in the structures was incredible. Ancestors proved to have superior intelligence. Within the castle, security was built to shield the community, with the ability to get into space swiftly. The material used to build the castle was from another dimension because the material could not be created again.

The substance was discovered long ago. The overlay material covered several types of marble stone, which sank into the walls and held the stones without using any type of connection. The circular design of the ceiling had a fourth- dimensional flow into a never-ending extended steeple.

Tepa's favorite place in the castle was standing underneath the steeple in the middle of the library floor. She looked directly into the flow of the opening in the ceiling, watching steadily as the space around the long steeple began to get smaller. Every day during her walk, Tepa attempted to hold her position, anticipating the very end of the design.

Instead, moisture swelled up, and mist fell from the steeple. The light moisture falling from the high steeple on her face caused her to move away from it.' The mist buildup stopped Tepa from examining the steeple. Being full of excitement, she said, "Just imagine, the unsighted end of the steeple could continue to a distant place." On her daily walk through the library, Tepa enjoyed and admired the sculptures aligned throughout the hallways. She saw the "No Visitors" sign at the end of the hallway, which was a signal for Tepa to start back. No one was supposed to go past it.

The sign had been there for as long as she could remember. But today, Tepa felt like she had been told enough about what she should or should not do. Feeling full of prerogative, Tepa saw no one else in sight and realized that she was alone. Normally, there was always someone around the corner or sitting and reading in the library, but not today.

It was the day of the town celebration, and everyone was attending the event. This time alone had created an open door for her, and she planned to take full advantage of this time. Tepa decided this was a good day to ignore the sign, so she walked past it. Her curiosity overcame her reasoning. She found herself on the other side of the "No Visitors" sign in front of the forbidden entry gate.

Tepa's heart began to beat fast with anxiety, and as her hand touched the antique handle of the gate, she gave a slight cringe caused by the coldness from the metal stone as she grasped the handle. Nervously, she tried to open the gate door and began to imagine that anything could happen to her.

She remembered the stories told about the castle. Such as the alien race disappearing, never to be seen again, and other stories she dares not to think about. Even though she remembered the remarks from others, gossiping about the myths of danger and the castle's mysteries, her determination was fueled to press forward. Tepa was not convinced to stop.

With closed eyes, she pulled the heavy gate completely open, leading her to an interior space. When Tepa stepped through, she found herself in an interior space that resembled an elevator without controls. Tepa expected more and felt extremely disappointed and defeated, which caused her to lay back on the wall of the interior space and fall through into a chamber.

Frightened by the unexpected fall, the startling drop to the floor alarmed her, but she regained her composure and cautiously moved forward, trying to comprehend what had just happened." Bewildered by the fall, she had to examine herself while still in the interior space, and when Tepa thought about it, she began laughing hysterically.

She laughed uncontrollably and was caught off guard hearing her echo of laughter, and the loud echo caused her to become frightened. Surprised and feeling fear at the same time, she became ecstatic to be a part of an amazing discovery.

"I cannot believe what I have missed," said Tepa, thinking if she would have known sooner, especially the camouflaged material. "I would have never believed if someone told me this type of material existed."

Anxious to see more, she quickly continued to move forward, needing to find answers and understand what had just happened. She was filled with many questions about the hidden area. Looking out among the dark hall, Tepa noticed there was another entrance in front of her, a large door. Focused and determined to finish what she started; she told herself not to turn back now. Yet, as she approached the large door, she questioned if she should enter. There were no locks on the door. She only had to push it open. Summoning her courage, she pushed against the door, feeling an opposing force on the other side. After a struggle, the door finally gave way.

She was now stepping out boldly into the unknown. The door was open, and she walked in. Tepa was extremely nervous, constantly talking to herself, and used her parent's words to continue, saying aloud, "You must grow up and be brave. Well, this is the time."

Inside, she was met by the glimpse of four extended spiraling staircases soaring so high she could not see the ending; it was flowing into infinity. There were no signs of a landing or a balcony in sight. Seeing and being in this place, chills began to start down her spine. Tepa, had a flurry of thoughts flowing through her mind, continued meditating and praying. Despite the fear bubbling within her, she refused to be held back.

She was determined to uncover the secrets that lay hidden from her, questioning the motives behind hiding the castle's structure and how much more was not seen by closing off areas to everyone, especially her.

Chapter Five

NO TURNING BACK

Determined to continue, Tepa saw a map on the floor of this enormous room, with light flickering throughout the structure, curves, and lanes on the floor, highlighting streams to plotted signs and numbers. She was intrigued and followed the directions to each stairway.

The stairs looked ancient and looked as if they had just been built. Each staircase had a railing light on the left and right, and the light went dark as she passed each staircase. Tepa entered one of the opening staircases and followed it. As she began the winding steps, she found herself in front of a deep curve.

The passage wall looked like other parts of the castle, with altered images showing the universe, stars, and other planets. A significant difference was the wall looked newer and had never been traveled through by anyone. The stones on the wall were shiny like gold, with no evidence of being touched by life.

Following one of the open passages inside the stairway, her body started to become faint, and she was feeling lightheaded, probably because the air was getting thinner, making it extremely hard to get air in her lungs. Tepa speaking out loud, "I can manage this, It is my only problem at the moment". Feeling confident she continued to move up the stairway. Breathing got easier.

She floated up the stairs and lost control of her abilities while moving swiftly up the stairway. Something is wrong. She could tell that she was moving fast and seemed to be extremely far away from the floor of the library entrance.

She was concerned about time and attempted to rethink the length of time spent in the room, and while moving upward on the staircase, she thought, how long have I been away from the main library? Despite her mounting anxiety, she knew at this point that turning back was no longer an option.

Tepa notice a deep curve coming forward, her body continue a fast speed in the stairway, she could not slow down.

She became fearless and more determined of the outcome to

reach the curve. Not knowing what she would find, she built up herself to be prepared. Tepa wondered when and where the stairway would end. As she turned into the curve, she was glad to see the floor was flat. She was able to walk, and her body felt normal again.

Moving extremely slowly, she was able to remain in control, which she needed to do just in case she needed to hide. Walking was so much easier, and suddenly, right in front of her, was a door that looked like glass. Tepa thought, not another door.

Through her journey so far, Tepa made mental notes of how she entered the passages, realizing that touching the entrances with both hands granted access. Deep down, she believed that every step she had taken so far was meant to happen and was not a coincidence.

The encounters of the day caused Tepa to become full of emotions. Tears began to rise and flow from her eyes, not knowing until she wiped her face. Knowing she was oblivious to what lay ahead weighed heavy in her thoughts. Tepa moved from her own feelings into more of a trance. She felt a push inside herself to witness what was behind the door. On the stone wall, she pushed a button, hoping the door would open, but the door did not.

Tepa stood boldly, showing confidence, and laid both of her hands directly on the door, and suddenly, it opened. As the door opened, she was extremely careful of her footsteps. If only she knew how seriously her next step would influence her destiny and others. The door slid open, and Tepa stepped onto a slightly medium-high platform. The platform was the beginning of the entrance to a wide, dark, warm hallway.

As she walked inside the space between the two walls, she noticed shadowy movements and something touching her face. Not knowing what was over her head or in front of her gave her a horrifying thought of the many types of insects that could be on her. She began to shake her body and wipe her face furiously. She felt a silky, translucent veil drop before her, touching her shaking hands. As she continued to move forward through the shimmering material, the atmosphere around her changed quickly to strong, intense, freezing winds.

Tepa buffeted her face with an emerald-beaded shawl she wore around her when she took her daily walks through the library. The wind became almost unbearable. Her curiosity had led her into a realm beyond her control, and now she found herself unable to retreat or move forward.

She saw a small opening further ahead of her. As she got closer, the opening became larger. She wondered what the opening led to, and at that moment, without any warning, an immense force took hold of her and heaved her body. She tried not to scream. But she screamed as loudly as she could, saying, "Something has me; somebody, please help me!"

The next tug from this force propelled her out through the lighted opening and into the cold void of space. Screaming and struggling to maintain her balance, she finally gained control. Tepa realized she was suspended in the vastness of space and rotating her body around to examine her surroundings.

She spotted the opening from which she was ejected. The edge of the opening was circled, with a long strap that hung for someone to use to pull themselves in. She said, as if anyone could hear her, "The strap had not been any help to me when I was suddenly expelled into space."

Gazing into the abyss, Tepa noticed a distant light in the vastness of space growing closer by the second toward her. Panic gripped her as she witnessed the light hurtling toward her at an alarming speed. Suddenly, she was grabbed with incredible swiftness, feeling as though she was being attacked.

The sheer quickness of her movement left her breathless, and thoughts raced through her mind. She refused to believe that this would be her demise, and no one would know or be aware of her whereabouts, and suddenly, darkness claimed her consciousness.

Tepa regained her senses, and found herself suspended in space, her waist secured by a wide band. Her hands were tucked within the band, providing her with enough freedom to move them. Clueless about what had transpired, she was immensely relieved to regain control over her hands. Using them to pull herself toward the opening, she made her way back into the passage, casting frequent glances into space to ensure nothing was coming after her.

She thought about what had happened to her. Although she did not understand how she was rescued, Tepa remembered noises and voices. She courageously fought to wake up but could not open her eyes to see. She felt no control of her body, like a terrible nightmare. Even listening to the voices was hard; her mind was clouded, and she could not hear clearly but found herself hanging in space. With a mixture of anxiety and determination, Tepa reentered the opening and urgently sought to seal it shut, pressing a button on the side of the wall until it closed.

Tepa did not know what to think about what had just happened. The passageway down the stairway was quicker. She was pushed down by the force of wind behind her with the ability to control her moves. As she hurried down the stairway, pulling the rails, it left a feeling of strength that she had never felt before. She also became bolder, but she was still frightened. She closed the door and returned to the hidden wall in the interior that looked like an elevator. Tepa placed the cover over the opening to make it invisible again.

Although she was alarmed by what had taken place, she wondered if her parents knew about what she had just seen.

Tepa hurried back to her room. She decided not to tell anyone for fear of not knowing what could happen. Tepa kept to herself what she had learned. She fell asleep, not noticing how dry the flowers in her vase were, proving Tepa was gone for days, not hours. As time passed, she decided it was a clever idea to keep this experience to herself and not talk about it to anyone. Her focus was to prepare for her grandfather's visit.

Chapter Six

SEASON OF CELEBRATIONS

The season of celebration began when all tribal communities met on planet Aralia, in the old land called Mount Trios, a place known for its extensive gems that shone so brightly and were seen in the universe. The gems were full of healing powers that merged into the aliens' genetics, creating stronger spiritual, mental, and physical abilities.

There was a stimulating power in the old land of Mount Trios, generating an atmosphere for joy and dancing. The food was why so many came to taste every type of cuisine from other universal planets. Of course, the main event was the invitation to the castle for new visitors and invited guests.

Tepa was very anxious, anticipating her grandfather's visit. He traveled for prolonged periods of time and visited every year during the Season of The Star's celebration. Tepa's parents were responsible for regulating and organizing the event, which kept them terribly busy hosting it. In previous years, Tepa complained often because she was too young to participate in any celebrations. Now that she was sixteen, she could take part in all the activities. Tepa's participation in the celebration would not interfere with her grandfather's visit.

She appreciated and enjoyed spending time with him and would never give up special moments of him reading to her. When she was a young girl, in the warm seasons, she would lie in the large rock fireplace. During the cold seasons, they sipped on golden hot and other warm drinks in front of the enormous fireplace. It comforted them from the cold breeze that traveled

through the castle.

Grandfather brought special books with him about mysterious things, but somewhere in the story, Tepa would always fall asleep hearing his constant heavy voice. It never failed. His voice would put her to sleep while reading to her. Her grandfather hoped she could still hear and dream about the stories. Tepa would always wake up early the next morning to tell her grandfather that "she dreamed about the stories and felt she were there".

As years passed, her grandfather's visits seemed more urgent.

He enjoyed spending time with her and teaching her about his travels. This time, her grandfather arrived with a special book to share. He hoped that this visit with his granddaughter would show him that she was ready for what was in store for her. This book was not an ordinary book, but a story that should awaken the origin of life, which connected to the planet Aralia, waking Tepa to her birthright.

Tepa dreamed about her experience in the hidden staircase that slung her into outer space and had been searching for answers. So, when she saw a view of him entering the room, she became eager and optimistic about the book her grandfather was carrying. She observed how he walked with pride with the book held in the upper part of his arm. His forehead was wet from sweating, which brought back memories of how her grandfather perspired when he was extremely uneasy.

As he walked closer to her, he took his handkerchief from his jacket to quickly remove the sweat from his brow. The airy castle gave way to secret smells that could not stay hidden. As the wind current flowed through the castle, Tepa smelled the familiar tobacco from his handkerchief. She smiled at her grandfather because she loved the smell of his pipe.

Although the smell caught her attention, she focused on the book, holding onto a great feeling of high expectancy. She could not wait to listen to the stories, which had become so important. Tepa glazed upon the item in her grandfather's hands. A book in a special leather case covered with colorful art designs. Words flowed through the cut ridge designs. On the front of the book, words moved actively within the designs.

Tepa connected the designs on the outside of her grandfather's book to the words on the wall that were positioned at the opening of the library and the walls in Tepa's amazing bedroom. Not forgetting the hallway of the ancient stairway, she found in the library's hidden cosmos location. Tepa thought, clearly, that the book was connected to countless answers. She was anxiously waiting to listen.

She looked at her grandfather with starry eyes, giving him full attention and waiting for the words that would come from his mouth. Tepa was like a baby bird waiting to be fed by his mother. He smiled at her, knowing what she had to be feeling. He was aware of the time Tepa spent in the library's hidden room and inside the first staircase, which changed her life. Her grandfather always believed that Tepa would find her pathway, especially when she faced opportunities that presented themselves.

Grandfather watched her mature over the years, all while observing and looking for signs of the ancestor gene, and after her time in the cosmos room, he sensed her power growing.
He always believed she was special. Her grandfather's essence of physical strength and spiritual being was overpowering, especially his remarkable appearance of aging.

His reputation of secret particular characteristics has been observed while on missions, as he taught leaders who had extraordinary gifts. He traveled throughout the galaxies to solve issues. Tribal aliens had to keep the planet safe. His ongoing involvement and experience in the universe had seen evil arising.

Tepa's grandfather opened the special book. She was still apprehensive and thought about what she would learn today.
She thought, could this book bring more surprises about my ancestor's family secrets? This would cause her to reveal to her grandfather how she found the hidden room in the library. She had never felt the way

she felt now. It was like everything she believed she knew about her life would never be the same again.

Grandfather explained how he found the book in a secret vault while looking for information about the Season of the Stars celebration. The inner room where he found the book was the oldest part of the castle, where no one was allowed in, not even Tepa's father, who was her grandfather's son. It had been said the inner room was the place where information about the ancestors was stored and how they disappeared. Tepa's curiosity led her to doubt her grandfather was looking for old art in the inner room of the attic in the castle.

He said, "Sharing this book with you will be the first time the story is shared with the new generation," sharing with her that she was the only one allowed to hear these words for hundreds of years to teach her about her ancestors. He hoped that Tepa would not allow fear to sway her from learning what was happening in the universe nor interfere with the ability to listen to the calling inside her.

That night, Tepa gave her grandfather total attention because she did not want to miss any of the story. He opened the book and began to read, with a slight smile on his face because his granddaughter

was sitting by him, holding onto his leg eagerly, anticipating and

hearing every word that came out of his mouth as he began to read

with his Aralia accent, an accent hardly ever heard.

Chapter Seven

THE STORY: PART ONE

The life cycles of planets are connected to each and every being in the universe. It is amazing how we have lived and performed for millions of years," said Tepa's grandfather. "We are amid new planets evolving constantly in the galaxy.

You will learn this night how frequently clusters form into planets within hundreds and thousands of dimensions to create lives and display spiritual illuminations.

Exquisite views of surrounding stars, waiting for transition to become part of a magnificent array of clusters. The creation of vibrant colored light generates seasons of enchantment awaiting a specific time to take place in space.

"During the span of time, the universe unlocked instruments developed in ancient times, created by intelligent ancient beings to secure the alien communities. A particular instrument, the realm, marvelously made, is a sight to see as Realms move slowly into motion and take over space with control, safety, and grace.

To watch the transition of the Realms opening is a remarkable sight, stars gleaming, in line with each other in the cosmos. Dust clouds with tiny particles make their way and set in the Milky Way, sprinkling themselves among the planets and creating a beauty that words cannot describe. Among all this beauty is the reason for the Season of the Stars.

"The universe is at its most vulnerable state during the Season of the Stars. Warriors perform their strength and prepare for the evil aliens, who are preparing for the battle that takes place between good and evil. The Season of the Stars brings the battles to a place away from the inhabitants of the planets. The battles between good and evil are about justice and judgment in the galaxies. The Season of the Stars protects evil from destroying the tribal warrior race.

Every year, the Season of the Stars commands warriors to the Realms of planets to protect inhabitants from evil adversaries hidden throughout outer parts of the Realms. Warriors travel from their planets with great speed into battles throughout the universe, tearing down the strongholds of evil barriers.

The warrior's body structure is built to conquer any evil alien in their pathway, using strength like that of the angels and supernatural skills. Their purpose is to fight and win the battle to subdue evil. When the battle ends, the warriors travel back to their planets. The Realms closes, and the universe is calm again, and planets are protected."

Grandfather smiled as he observed Tepa's involvement in listening to the story. He continued to bring her into the story of what had come and what was now. "In the aftermath of the old wars, time seems to move slowly. Future wars are destined to end for the sake of the universe. Warriors establish an rules to keep the planets safe and in control. Deliberate sanctions were placed to monitor the whereabouts of their enemies.

As the universe actively expands, and as years pass, changes take place, what was before is no more. Nothing stays the same. The power of energy creates signals and secrets, which are hidden among the stars and stay hidden until the chosen time reveals itself.

During the past years, the Season of the Stars occurred much more often, with high fatalities from the evil aliens who were willing to do anything to take over the universe.

Aware that if evil ever won a battle, the planets would suffer the loss in their way of living. Having to live through more wars and deaths, evil would make living unbearable. The warriors understand their strategy and how evil searches for ways to conquer and reach the planets and then the inhabitants.

In this year of the Season of the Stars. The malicious determination of the evil aliens to win the war began by disregarding all the rules and conditions set by the warriors. The evil aliens secretly launched war schemes and made decisions to ensure the changes made would give them the greatest opportunity to capture the warrior's communities successfully.

"Although these actions would cause a high consequence to the death of many evil aliens, who had no care in their hearts for each other and willingly sacrificed their teams.

The evil aliens built smaller crews, knowing these crews would be killed when they were sent out to fight the warriors. Leaving fewer of them to fight in the battle, committing the other teams to proceed to the hidden plan as the battle took place. "Just as the war was happening with the warriors, a group of evil aliens tried to enter the realm of the warrior's planet. The first time evil went against the realm's rules for entering unprotected planets during wartime.

The warriors were unaware of plots made to change the outcome of the battle with them. As the evil aliens began to enter the Realms of the planet, an extremely cold force of air pressure in the realm caused injury and death to some of the evil team. It was almost impossible for them to enter, but they did enter and began to launch an attack.

The battle of good and evil was now at maximum force, totally absorbing every corner to keep the evil alien visible in the universe. The warriors had no suspicion of the small number of evil alien teams during the battle. Therefore, they had no reason to concern themselves for the planet's safety, not knowing of an attack.

Amusingly, the evil aliens observed the relentless heart of the warrior tribal race as they protected their planet. They were blocking the entry, fighting with a skill of efficacy, showing no intention to give up their planet. They realized that they loss the advantage to defend the planet, the warrior's tribe began to take the next step. It was an important next step to ensure protection for the tribal aliens on the planet, with the determination not to lose hope.

While evil aliens proceeded to destroy the tribal aliens and take the planet, they weakened the defense structure defended by the tribal warriors. The warrior's tribal race was one of a kind, with a heart of survival, with many generations of fighting and allegiance in their genetic material.

The tribes had no fear nor intention of giving the evil alien control of their planets. Although the evil aliens had broken through the realm of one of the planets, they were feeling confident and believed their evil plan was working.

In the universe battle, the warriors were fully engaged, removing as many evil aliens as possible. Their focus was to protect their planets, and they were preoccupied with the ease of clearing the war spaceship with hundreds of evil aliens. No one noticed the evil aliens had fewer armies.

For sure, the warriors never expected them to move differently, and there was no way to know that the aliens planned to attack the home planets.

"As the aliens attacked with brutal and fierce force, they were surprised and could not understand how the tribal race was surviving. Evil aliens misjudged the warrior's alien race. The warrior tribe already knew how the fight would end because they were in charge of their destiny and understood the larger picture, the responsibility for the entire universe.

The planets were about to be completely overthrown by the enemy. The tribal leaders took immediate action and began the security protocol countdown to destroy their planet. Through determination and commitment, the tribal leader's predicament led them to destroy their own planet and sacrifice their alien race before allowing the evil aliens to have them and their planet. The team started the security protocol as quickly as they could.

"The first protocol was to send as many of the tribal aliens as possible to a place where they would wait for rescue. The second protocol was to begin the security countdown to destroy the planet before the enemy took control of the planet.

"They began to fill the spaceships with the warrior's children and elders. Anyone left would perish with the planet. And hopefully, some of the evil aliens. As the spaceships with special cargo took off, the planet was destroyed. It was sensed throughout the universe.

During the battle, the warriors saw an explosion in the universe among the many Old-World planets. Their hearts dropped, knowing, but they never wanted to believe it was one of their planets. They hoped the security protocol for the planet was followed, leaving enough time to get everyone off the planet.

Meanwhile, spaceships carrying valuable cargo made it off the planet and were now in space. Evil aliens spotted the spaceships flying from the broken planet. One particular ship clad with symbols was significantly larger than the other spaceships. The enemies made haste and intercepted the special spaceship, capturing children, elders, and other precious items.'

After taking the spaceship, they swiftly rushed to enter their planet's galaxy deep in the universe. Although the evil aliens lost the battle with the warriors, unknowingly, they stole the most important alien race from the warriors. "The warriors were focused and determined, refusing to let anger or fear control their feelings and waiting for confirmation.

The message they were waiting for came. They were told that one of the spaceships was intercepted by the evil aliens. The warriors made a pact and did not pause or stop at anything.

"Ominously searching and preparing to recover them, they discovered traces of fumes. The fumes from the emission of the evil alien's spaceship. In space, fumes generate dusty paths like a dusty road on land. The difference was the dusty path in space that lasted for days, which was all the warriors needed to trace the evil alien.

Finally, a confirmation of the pathway the evil aliens' rode. Once they acknowledged the evidence was firm, the warriors started to follow the pathway. They hoped to find survivors from the demolished planet. It was an agonizing wait. Warrior's spaceships followed the particles of dust, leading them straight to the evil aliens. Found deep in the galaxy of the Milky Way in outer space, there was a hazy light over the stars caused by the dark covering from the evil fog.

As the warriors moved through space following the misty path left from the spaceship, darkness surrounded them, and there was a feeling of coldness and hopelessness all around them. This feeling reminds the warriors why they fight.

"In this part of the galaxy, the light was hidden. Only darkness lived in this part of the universe now.'

"The warriors from every planet in the universe came together as a team to retrieve the kidnapped aliens using their strength together. They agreed to attack with force and change the galaxy from darkness.

A universally recognized, elite group of pursuit air force tracked the aliens and found the planet holding the abducted. They notified the warriors of an Old-World planet inhabited by aliens full of evil. "After the warriors were signaled, they came into the battle, and they moved with swift vigor. Their focus was to retrieve the warrior's tribes without losing any of them. They heard the cries from the ground. The evil aliens split the youth from the older aliens, and the young ones retaliated ferociously that the sounds flowed from their vocal cords into the air.

This made the warriors fight harder and quicker to remove this evil from the universe as soon as possible. They fought the enemy with the pursuit team with vigor. The evil aliens struggled to get control of the fight because they were caught off guard.

The universe had lost countless great, gifted aliens from

their tribes, taken by evil, not knowing where they were. This time, the warriors would not stop until the aliens were pushed back to where they came from. They forced the aliens toward an open gate in the universe, and the pursuit team took control, proceeding to ensure the captured evil aliens were behind the gates so they could be watched. This was a move to secure future movements because it seemed they always found a way to come back.

The pursuit team that went in with the aliens was pulled into the abyss as they pushed the evil aliens through the gate. While in the abyss, pursuit teams saw structures and evidence of other life forms and decided to follow the enemy's path, which led them to the largest structure. While hiding, they saw tribal aliens living under guard, a group of aliens that looked like kings and others with a presence about them.

Thinking while looking at each other with the face of alarm, we could not speak. They could not chance the evil aliens hearing them. They witnessed tribal aliens dressed in royalty clothes as a sign of importance.

The pursuit team had to leave to return another time because there was no way to fight the evil aliens without getting captured. Although feeling very sure of seeing missing leaders and others held hostage, they had to leave them and return another time to save them."

Chapter Eight

Survival for the Warrior Alien Race

Meanwhile, the warriors wiped out the evil aliens from the planet where the hostages were. The warriors had a dilemma. Whether or not to allow the inhabitants who were brought to the planet long ago to continue to live on the planet. "They had to decide what to do with their warrior tribal aliens. Their planet was destroyed, and the other planets would have to make space for the survivors.

The only choice left was to settle the survivors among the original inhabitants on the Old-World planet. They did not question if this was a promising idea. Hmmm, maybe they should have! "Expectations were extremely high among the warriors as they changed evilness in space to an atmosphere of good presence.

Commuting to and from the galaxies within the universe, areas where evil laid hold and corrupted the Old- World planets in the deep part of the galaxy changed quickly. "With help from powerful beings, the mask of evil that was placed upon this once beautiful planet was removed. Warriors from the demolished planet stayed on the Old-World planet to protect the survivors.

"As years passed, the warriors lived on the top of the highest mountain. They changed the planet's atmosphere as they opened the realm to let lights and spirituality flow throughout the planet. Warriors constructed magnificent tall buildings to enter the Realms and universe. They brought back the life of planet Aralia and lived by these words. 'Goodness Is in The Midst of Power.'

"The warriors did not realize how much the original inhabitants living among the evil aliens could not change their evil innate ways. They no longer knew good after their king brought his tribes to Aralia and left them on the planet, to never return, because the angels sent him into a black hole to control the true evil using him, and now the new alien tribes are left to live with these evil aliens. This caused fear and problems among the children of the warriors.

"The fate of the tribal aliens left to live on this planet will feel like the end, having a heart-breaking reality of watching their elder leaders suffer and die trying to conform to the way of living among the old inhabitants and the animals. The lack of the elderly's experience and knowledge to teach them who they were as tribal aliens would be missed.

The young alien warriors had no memories of what they knew of their ancestors because the elders did not survive long on the planet. The young aliens never knew the warriors who watched over them existed. Oblivious to the fact that the warriors watched over them on top of the highest mountain.

"It was not easy for the young aliens, but they naturally knew how to care for themselves. Imagine a group of young aliens learning how to stay safe from the inhabitants, animals, and evil aliens. They stayed together in fear of the original inhabitants and learned how to survive the Old-World planet. Throughout generations, the Old-World planet became the place where they would learn their power and purpose in the universe."

Chief Amasis

"Below the high mountains, the original inhabitants lived on plains, and they were more adept to the turbulent environment on the planet. The warrior's descendants were the tribal alien race. They learned from experiences and tragedies on the planet and remembered some of their memories from the elders as they got older and learned to pass alone to each other, never forgetting their ancestors' stories.

"The Old-World aliens caused fear among the tribal aliens, but there was one who would not be intimidated by the original inhabitants. He was fearless and became a leader among the alien race of the tribes. His name was Amasis.

"Tribes looked to Amasis for guidance and wisdom, and they chose him to be the tribal chief. Chief Amasis taught the tribal aliens how to build strength and find power within themselves. He taught them to fight for it. He was a great leader and encouraged the tribes to follow the rules of the council. He said to them, 'If you follow the rules created for all the tribes, you will build strength, grace, honor, morality, and goodness for the good of us all.'

"The tribes were mindful and followed the teachings of Chief Amasis for protection. Taking this responsibility created a bond among them. He always reminded the tribal aliens that 'Goodness is a key to great power,' something he remembered from the elders.

"The tribes worked together to feed their families. Weapons were built to protect them from the original inhabitants and animals. Chief Amasis warned the tribes to be watchful of the original inhabitants of the plains. He explained that they were an evil alien race with evil intent and as dangerous as the animals that existed. The tribes were cautious and eager to keep watch over each other.

"The original alien inhabitants were led with the reminisce of evil aliens, which are their children. Throughout the land, hate is carried in their hearts. The tribal aliens knew nothing about the original alien race. Only the rumors heard among the tribes. That the eyes of the original alien race were cold, and they carried

wickedness in their essence. They were very evil, not caring about

their life. They fought among themselves for survival.

"The original inhabitant's intention was to live an evil life.

They knew no other way to live. They roamed Aralia to destroy and

attack tribes. They were called the original alien race because they

were the first aliens who lived on the planet after the battle between

kings, which caused evil to awaken in the universe and tried to

destroy everything good. They had secrets of skills to subdue and kill

Old-World animals, which are fierce, deceiving, and evil.

"The original alien race used knowledge that was passed to

them within generations. It was said the leader of the original alien

race moved through dimensions from planets, and evil spread and

overtook the planet, leaving the evil alien race of original

inhabitants. The leader had not been seen since. This type of evil

alien leader had roamed the universe with the only purpose of

looking for souls to take.

"Although the original alien race was fearless, they had a fear

of Chief Amasis. For unknown reasons, the original alien race never confronted tribal aliens protected by the chief. Chief Amasis recognized that the original inhabitants avoided him. Understanding this gave him the boldness to bring other tribes under his protection.

"The chief has always had a concern for the tribes outside of his protection. He said, 'Come and abide with our tribes because one day you will lose to the original inhabitants or the animals because of your vulnerability.' But the tribe wanted to live with fewer aliens.

"Chief Amasis was full of thoughts and constantly pondered the concerns of the other tribes who were farther away from his tribes. He saw the problem of time, knowing that if help was needed during a season, no one could make it to help them because they were out of his reach. He was speaking of the secured their tribes from the secured their tribes from the inhabitant animals."

"Now, the chief had to wait to travel to the other tribes until the animal grazing season was over, and the valley was safe when the animals moved back to the plains. Now, it was too late to travel."

Grazing Season

"During the grazing season, the animals roamed in packs, looking for food. It was called the grazing season because the animals would stay at times for months to feed on the tribal aliens. This was a season when the animals were allowed to graze along the edge of the tribal land. If they saw and came close enough to any of the tribal aliens, they would attack and feed on them with help from the original inhabitants.

"During the last few grazing seasons, the animals could not feed on many, and that was because of Chief Amasis, who taught the tribes to stay in the protected areas during the grazing season. The tribal aliens were secure among each other. No one went out during the season of grazing.

"Chief Amasis also taught the tribes to keep food stored for their families. The animals stayed for days, waiting to capture someone to feed on. There was always someone from the tribe who thought they were safe enough to leave the area and be captured by going out too far from the tribe.

"One morning, during the season of animal grazing, the tribal aliens were awakened. Something was happening with the animals, making horrendously high-pitched sounds. At the same time, the packs far away were making the same sound.

"Chief Amasis remembered a time when he heard these same sounds from the horrid animals. He thought the animals were next to him, but they were far away. Their sounds traveled with the wind, miles across the plains. Listening to the animals brought up a childhood memory to Chief Amasis of a terrible experience that he had forgotten about, one he encountered when he was a child when he saw the real evil of the animals and their cunningness and intelligence.

"He was with one of the elders, who lost their life protecting him. The elder heard the animals' pitch, calling the other animals. He thought they were close behind them, and so he led young Amasis to travel forward. They were far away from the tribe.

"A little time passed; the elder thought he had moved fast enough to lose the animals behind them. Moving forward, he realized it was a trick because they came face-to-face with the animals. The elder did not know what to do. The animal's treachery showed on its face, with a look of pridefulness.

"Chief Amasis would never forget how they tortured the elder before killing him to eat. As the animals put the elder's body to the side, they looked at him and began to move forward. But a sudden sound, very loud, brought winds and thunder around young Amasis, and the ground trembled, causing the animals to flee.

"Chief Amasis tried to see what was behind him. He was so brave and not afraid. The air was filled with thick dust, and he could not see. As a little boy, he only knew to run; he ran so hard, not stopping, and ran right into the middle of the tribal prayer for the elder and him.

"As he grew up, he knew that they were not alone. Learning how the original inhabitants imitated the sounds of animals, he knew they communicated with the inhabitant animals.

"Chief Amasis watched how the animals suddenly moved away from the tribes, leaving sooner than the normal grazing time. He knew something was happening to make them leave. When the animals moved away from the Amasis tribes, they moved toward the tribes living on the other side of the plains.

The tribes did not understand the animals were following the call from the original inhabitants. It was the way the original inhabitants communicated with them. Chief Amasis figured it out and was concerned about what was going to happen.

"The original inhabitants terrorized the tribes who were far from the protection of Chief Amasis. While taking control of the tribal aliens, the Old-World inhabitants punished the tribes that were lost to Chief Amasis, taking their belongings and all of their possessions and banishing them from their homes, sending them into the plains. the old inhabitants controlled the animals, by feeding them."

Chapter Nine

THE STORY: PART TWO

Chief Amasis prepared to make a journey to urge other tribal aliens to join his tribes.

Before he could travel, he was told about the tragedy across the plains. The scouts saw the attack on the tribal aliens by the original inhabitants. "He hoped it was not too late to help them, but the tribes had already been banished, punished, and had their belongings stolen by the original inhabitants. The chief understood and could only hope they would try to escape the animals and cross the plains to the Amasis tribes.

"Chief Amasis's response was quick. He summoned brave men and women to scout the plains. The scouts were told to look for the tribes who were attacked and banished by the original inhabitants and to bring them to Amasis land.

"The scouts discovered the tribes and learned they were attacked and killed by the animals of the plains. Chief Amasis was deeply saddened by the news. He thought about the suffering of the tribes and how they had to endure the animal's torture. He described to the tribes how the inhabitant animals killed. He said the saliva in the animal's mouth carried a poison that killed slowly, causing extreme pain when bitten, and if the poison did not kill their prey, the acid from the animal's skin would."

Heart Broken

"Angry for losing so many tribes, Chief Amasis understood that one day, the animals would eventually attack every tribe, and no one would survive because the animals would kill until all the prey was dead. He could see clearly how, ultimately, the original alien race, or the animals, would wipe out everyone. Chief Amasis believed staying in the valley of the plains was not an option anymore. The only choice left was to leave and take the tribes to a safer place.

"Chief Amasis had a great imagination of the power on the

mountaintop. It fascinated him and gave him hope. The strong vibration and echo from the mountain were one thing, but the displays of light, thunder, and stars on top of the mountain day and night proved that something or someone was living there, right on the mountain top.

The activity and reflections he saw at night made him want to see further into the sky and mountains. His curiosity grew stronger than ever. The chief felt he must know what or who was making the noises heard so far away in the mountains. There was no doubt the sounds were from above on the mountaintop.

"The chief, feeling a connection to the mountain ranges, never shared his feelings with the tribes of his visions, believing one day, he would understand the force pulling him to the risks of the mountains. He dreamed the same dream often, climbing to the mountaintop and finding this great celebration.

"Chief Amasis genuinely believed there was something greater than him and the tribal alien race on top of the mountain. He studied for answers to save the tribes. Having the ability to see further would be the beginning of finding his answers. He knew the task was great. Finding a better way to see closer into the sky and the mountaintop would be an impossible task. Yet deep in his heart, Chief Amasis knew there was a way and believed he would find it.

"Chief Amasis, with patience, pondered and eagerly waited for the answer to come, and it had to be soon. He was concerned about the other leaders in the Amasis tribe. Although he was the chief and had the largest tribe among all the tribes, he allowed leaders of each tribe to join him as they continued to join him so all the alien races could be heard. He wonders if it was the right decision. However, Chief Amasis taught them an important message: to think for themselves, no matter what.

"Some tribes could not understand the chief's concern about death in the future if they did not find a way to leave. They said to Chief Amasis they felt safe and wanted to stay where they were. These tribes believed they could live where they were and not be hurt by the original alien race or the animals if they stayed among the tribes.

"Chief Amasis left the other leaders, debating in his head, thinking he had had enough of them speaking of fear. "His mind flooded with thoughts, and he was exhausted. He lay on his bed, sleep took over, and he went into a deep sleep. The chief was awakened from a dream that made his entire body wet from sweating during sleep. Sometimes, his dreams were hard to remember, but this dream became clear to Chief Amasis. He remembered everything about it.

"The chief, going over his dream, realized the dream was real and the alien beings in the dream were kings. The kings were having an intense conversation, talking among themselves, debating about significant matters while looking over at Chief Amasis's way. The chief perceived them discussing him because of the way they watched him. He heard them asking if it was him, and if it was, it must be time.

"As they looked upon Chief Amasis, they continued talking among themselves as if he were not there listening to them. The kings said, 'We have to make up for what we helped create many years ago in the universe, which has to start here and now.' Chief Amasis thought, is this dream real?"

"In his reality, they came to him because he could not walk to

them at first. Chief Amasis was shocked by the kings.
The only aliens in his life were the tribal alien tribes and the dark
inhabitants who he could barely see because they hid, and those who
had perished while they were young. He had never seen aliens like
these.

"The kings were positioned over Chief Amasis. They reached
down to pull him up, and once touched by them, something
happened inside him. He quickly realized it was no longer a dream
because he was completely capable of moving throughout space.
Gravity could not hold him. He moved through space above the
valley and the mountains into the universe. He soared through the
planets, stars, and universe and looked out into infinity. He was
introduced to ancient wars via visions on a large screen.

The chief saw the past. "Chief Amasis was filled with
knowledge, connecting him with ancestors and their past. He
discovered an evil greater than what he believed to have existed on
the Aralia planet; the malevolent dark ghost, once good, changed the
original inhabitants into who they became.

"The kings motioned for him to come, and he found himself

his body was still lying on the sleeping bed while he was walking. He now knew who the alien kings were after the history of the universe was shown to him while he was moving throughout the universe.

They showed him everything that happened on the day of King Odonias's disappearance. He felt heartfelt, and tears ran down his face as he realized who he was and what he had to do. Yet he was full of happiness to be with them.

"They took him to a place in the plains. The animals sensed them but never attempted to attack any of the kings. They carried a great power that genuinely created fear in the animals and the original inhabitants. So, the animals did not move because they could sense kings. They took him to a place where Chief Amasis saw a small mountain of displaced rocks.

When the rocks were removed, there was material folded neatly underneath, strange shiny and wafer-thin material. The chief had never seen anything like this. He knew there was something special about it."

The Dream Became a Vision

"It seemed like within a moment, he was back asleep, and when Chief Amasis awoke, it was early morning. He remembered his dream. He knew it was more than a dream, more than a vision. Quietly, Chief Amasis called to his soldiers quickly. After gathering them, Chief Amasis said, 'You are my most trusted, and I know you well. I trained each of you myself.

"'You now must trust me more than you ever have.' The soldiers were stunned by the chief's face, full of anxiety, sweat running from his brown skin, with the sweat from his forehead looking like drips of blood.

"They began to whisper among each other out of concern for the chief who was hoping that once he told them what he needed them to know; would change their lives forever and never be the same. These whispers became noticeable, and Chief Amasis realized he had to tell them about the vision.

"Afterward, the soldiers knew they had to help him because nothing nor anyone could take the vision off his mind. He shared with them the material he saw in his dream. He asked his soldiers to follow him to the plains and tell no one. He knew they would be safe. The soldiers asked no questions and did as they were asked because they trusted the chief.

"Chief Amasis led his soldiers to the plains. After a few hours of travel, he found the pile of rocks from his dream. At that moment, he knew his life had changed. He had no fear of anything. They helped him remove the pile of rocks and found the material in the same place. As he touched and held the pieces of material in his hands, he saw the same thin wafers of material in his dream.

He was amazed at the material that looked like glass, see-through glass. He held a piece up to the sky and could see deep into the universe and the mountains.

"When he returned to the tribe, Chief Amasis designed the tool he had been wanting for a long time. Once he finished it, he quickly used it to see closer into space. He used the new tool made of the material, the sky-watcher, to look in space and magnify high mountains day and night, revealing things Chief Amasis had not seen before.

"The signs from the sky rendered the Chief Amasis able to look closely. He believed that someone in the mountains could help all the tribes. He watched stars glistening and falling on Aralia, lighting up the mountains. Magnificent structures were showing up on the mountaintop as he watched during the day.

"Chief Amasis determined more now, with all the evidence, that the wait was over. He knew he must leave and take as many tribal people with him as possible when he departed. The tribal leaders had always agreed that no one would be forced to venture to the mountaintop. The chief thought for a moment about what it would take to get to the mountains without losing his tribe, but his strong belief assured him that they could make it.

Chief Amasis asked the soldiers to bring all the material they found underneath the rocks. It was more than enough material for everyone "Chief Amasis waited, and he wondered what was taking the soldiers so long to come back. He called out for them and was shaken by the sounds of the voices around him. It was his soldiers, and he could not see them. Only one of the soldiers laid down the material, and only then was the chief able to see him.

"All the soldiers began to lay down the material, and he could see all the soldiers. He knew this could only be a blessing from heaven. The chief had his answer and knew they would make it to the mountain top because they had protection from the animals.

Chief Amasis was not concerned about the original inhabitants. Obviously, the original inhabitants understood more about Chief Amasis's vision. They knew what was happening. Since the visitation in his dream, he had changed, and they knew it.

"The chief spoke to all the tribes about his dreams and vision of the kings, telling the tribal leaders he believed that the mountaintop was where they belonged to have a safe life. He announced to all the tribes, welcoming the tribes to come with him.

"The day he led the tribes out to the plains; he became disappointed because he left twelve chief leaders of tribal communities that reacted to him in fear and chose to stay. They told Chief Amasis that he would get everyone killed going to the plains. The tribal aliens were afraid of the animals because they were prey for them."

Freedom Pass Fear of the Animals

"The dangerous animals roamed the land, even more on the plains, away from the tribes. They were unbelievably larger than the tallest tree on the land. The problem was not just the large animals; the small animals were dangerous, too. The tribes realized that eating green vegetables and fruit was the only safe way to feed their tribes.

"The meat from fish, or mammoth, was not an option. Each tribe leader knew that the chances of killing fish or any type of animal would be a significant risk. They learned by losing many hunters and realized it was impossible to kill before they were killed.

"As Chief Amasis and his tribe headed to the plains and valley, they saw the animals roaming everywhere, more than they expected. At one point, they stood and waited to be ravaged by the animals, as they had done in the past. As they traveled, the chief and tribes were assured by the fact that the animals did not see them. Chief Amasis instructed each man, woman, and child to sew large pieces of wafer material to their clothes, and if they needed to hide totally, they just covered.

"They quickly moved forward. The large tribe was still in fear and was incredibly quiet. As they continued their journey, they found food to eat. The emotions shown by the chief revealed faith and belief that there was a greater presence among them, watching out for the tribes. He felt he made the right decision to follow his instinct.

"They traveled by day and at night slept. They felt positive by remembering how far they had come; they continued for months as the season changed. They gathered dry bushes and trees that had fallen from the breakage of animals roaming. They used the largest pieces to cover them while they slept.

"As they got closer to the mountains, the tribes remembered exactly how the sounds from the mountaintop were faint. They were heard throughout the night while sitting with their families and tribes around the roaring large fire.

"Now, the tribes were experiencing the effects from the rolling thunder under their feet as the ground shook from the active mountain: some felt the ground would open, and everyone would fall in. The roaring vibration and the flicking of the bright, blinding lights became disturbing for the tribes.

"The tribal leaders said they remembered the time spent in front of the fire with their families listening to the sounds heard from the mountain top as they flowed throughout the valley and plains but now being so close to the foot of the mountain, fear was rising among the tribes. The tribes wanted to turn around and go back, not knowing what was happening at the top.

"Chief Amasis said, 'Yes, you are afraid, but you must believe that everything that has happened is for our protection. There is a higher protection over us we cannot turn back. We must trust not in feelings but what you have experienced.' "'We have the opportunity to understand what is happening on the top of the mountains. It is our destiny.' Although the tribes could not see the structures, he knew what he had seen in his vision and understood that whoever or whatever was up there could protect the tribes.'

"Rain, thunder, and lightning in the valley was strong, but no match on the mountaintop. Chief Amasis, not discouraged, continued with his tribes to face whatever was on the top of the mountain.

"The valley was not safe for the tribes. They had no chance of life with the animals, for they were too large to run from or kill. Chief Amasis was determined to save the tribes from the animals and original inhabitants, and he convince the tribes to continue."

Chapter Ten

THE STORY: PART THREE BLESSING IN THE MIDST OF THE STORMS

Making the mountain climb became an unexpected task for the tribes for four long days and three cold nights. It was concerning how the enormous mountain elevation soared higher. It became so wide that it felt like a parallel forest, while everyone's only thought was the distance to reach the mountain top.

"The winds were blowing fiercely. They continued climbing, although he knew the tribes were in trouble. They could not take the cold winds and rain for much longer. They were slipping and trembling from the force of the strong rainfall. When Chief Amasis saw the impact of the weather on the tribes, he was concerned and continued to search for shelter.

As they climbed up the mountain, small caves were

strategically lined on the rocky side of the mountain.

One of the caves was beautiful and had a red door and a star. It was sitting oddly by itself and stood out among the others. Obviously, Chief Amasis believes this was an open invitation. He turned to face everyone with a smile and said," Faithful tribes, this is a symbol to the resolute tribes and reward for following me and exiting the horrid plane and evil low valley".

A light shone on a particular cave with an illuminating crystal surface pathway, which led to a large red door. Chief Amasis opened the door to the cave. He was startled with amazement because the cave was lit by fluorescent lights of enormous plants. Everyone could see as they walked into the cave. The cave opened into a room that seemed to become more sizable as the tribes entered in, creating enough room to fit every tribe. Everyone was stunned by the natural beauty in the cave, and at that moment, all the uncertainty the tribes had felt before became a reality, and leaving the valley was their destiny.

"Chief Amasis and his tribe found refuge within a mystical cave high up in the mountain. This unexpected secure sanctuary transformed their fortunes from a perilous struggle against the numerous elements to a refuge of wonder and greater abundance. The initial respect and gratitude began to intertwine with curiosity and a longing for how this was happening, creating the urgent need to understand the mysteries that surrounded them.

"The radiant glow of fluorescent lights from embedded gems and minerals continued to light their way within the cave. It was as if the stones of the mountain held a secret connection of energies of the universe, guiding them toward a mysterious destiny. The alien tribes marveled at the intricate fireplaces that adorned the walls, providing warmth and comfort in contrast to the harsh winds outside.

"Discovering deeper into the cave, they encountered chambers that were more than just comfort but found bountiful tables laden with assorted fruits and vegetables, which offered a feast that appeared to have sprung up from the ground itself. Laughter and songs filled the air; tribes shared the joy of their newfound haven. Standing with the other leaders, Chief Amasis smiled at their quick transformation from a once troubled and weary group now thriving in this underground sanctuary.

"Chief Amasis, feeling complete security for the tribes, opted to venture deeper into the cave and was drawn by the sound of rushing water." "Following a span of melodious notes of nature's symphony, stumbled upon a breathtaking sight. A waterfall cascaded from an opening in the ceiling, forming a shimmering pool of spring water.

The water continued its pattering journey through the ruins of the ancient cave, transitioning from cool to soothingly warm as it flowed over rocky terrain into a natural spa. The sight was a true testament to the harmonious blend of elements in this hidden realm. Nevertheless, the chief was compelled and explored further, sensing there was more to discover. He followed a narrow path behind the waterfall and began to hear a sound. As he focused more closely, a strangely familiar voice reached his internal hearing.

"Hearing the voice made Chief Amasis slowly take steps backward, feeling uncertain of what lay ahead. Questions swirled in his mind, of a quiet voice beckoning him forward, moving him to feel indescribable unease and curiosity. The chief bravely continued and stepped into a lighted concealed passageway, being convinced of the significance.

"The voice reassured him, saying it was safe for him to enter. 'You know who I am. You will remember again.'

"Chief Amasis reluctantly chose to trust the alien voice, and he continued. The roaring sounds of the waterfall faded as he followed the voice, wandering amid the jagged rocks, transformed into massive marble walls.

"Finally, reaching the entrance to a place in the mountain, the image appears impossible. He could not believe his eyes as he walked out into a community of tribal aliens living without fear. The leader approached him, and when he spoke, Chief Amasis recognized it as the voice that had led him there.

"The leader introduced himself as Moab, a tribal alien and one of the original inhabitants of Aralia. Chief Amasis looked around. There was no resemblance to the evil original inhabitants. Moab sought the best way to convince Chief Amasis of the intertwined true tales of ancient origins and interdimensional travel.

"He explained there was a time when angels lived on planets throughout the universe to safeguard and protect against all evil. At a time when angels engaged themselves in the lives of tribal people while living on various planets scattered throughout the vast universe. The noble mission was to safeguard and protect against all forms of evil that might arise.

"Moab studied Chief Amasis to observe his acceptance of what he had heard so far and continued with the true story of King Trios, a once good, powerful being. How he brought the tribal aliens to Aralia, a place of abundance and harmony. They lived in the valley and the plains years before the planet fell victim to evil forces.

"Moab explained how King Trios had brought them to this dimension where they were. Although it looked like they were still in the cave, they were really far removed from the mountain and its tribal aliens. Chief Amasis was eager to hear and listen carefully to understand how such things are possible. Moab elaborated on King Trios's connection to other dimensions and his quest to study the mighty kings of the universe.

"Despite his desire for a connection, the kings disrespected him, causing King Trios to withdraw his longing to engage in knowing them. The kings, unaware of the king's hidden power, mistakenly made the worst decisions. It was to disregard his attempts at communication. The lack of respect shown eventually provoked an unwanted revelation of hidden power in the hardened heart of King Trios.

"The Elder Kings built false confidence, not recognizing how blind they were by thinking that their combined strength and igniting power remained untouchable, keeping them ignorant of their false accomplishment. Not anticipating the unleashing of destruction upon the universe.

"King Trios gave the Elder Kings a fight they never expected. He returned and moved all of his tribes to the entrance of this dimension. He intended to return them safely back to their home planets. But he left them there intending to finish the fight with the Elder Kings. "Though, something transpired in him and consumed him with an unexpected spirit of darkness and desire. King Trios never returned. Evil consumed him, which led to the destruction of planets, including the beautiful Aralia.

"Moab's retelling of history filled Chief Amasis with awe and sadness. Moab continued, telling Chief Amasis how the approaching evil confrontation changed everything because the malevolent evil force trapped King Trios. Once the darkness began to shadow over the valley and plains, they could see great devastation in the universe.

"Moab said, 'We have been here waiting on a promise that you, Chief Amasis, and your companions will arrive one day and release us. It is time to restore what has been taken by evil and bring our king back to his universe.'

"Moab handed Chief Amasis a beautiful, armored sword made of an unknown material, found during the tribe's abduction during the warrior's war against evil aliens. Moab believed it was Chief Amasis's lost sword, a young alien holding it while the evil aliens chased him. He said, 'The sword possesses a power only you can unlock. With this sword in your hand, King Trios can be released.'

"Chief Amasis, fearless but deeply aware of his destiny, accepted the sword and stepped forward. He returned to his tribes, shared the story and prepared them for the impending battle. Their newfound haven had transformed into a sanctuary of training and resilience, where they honed their skills under Moab's guidance.

"The atmosphere was very full of determination as alliances were formed, and unity grew among the tribes in another dimension with the tribal aliens.

Finally, the destined night arrived, and Chief Amasis stood strong as a great warrior at the cave's precipice, gazing out at the valley that had once been their home. He held up his sword, lightning split the sky, thunder echoed similar to ancient war drums, and the ground trembled beneath their feet.

"Moab, and Chief Amasis, guided the tribes and recent allies with unwavering resolve, a beacon of hope in the midst of chaos. They moved into the deepest part of a world never seen before. When they approached, they saw a king battered with chains attached to his body. The evil malevolent had left him because he no longer had use for him.

"Moab called to his king, 'King Trios, we come for you.' The king replied with awakening joy, 'Moab, Gracious leader, you have come!'

"Come with us so we can be returned to our dimensions."

"You have wasted your time, for the only ones who can release me are the angels, and they don't know that I am free from the evil spirit.' At that very moment, a host of angels appeared.

Chief Amasis and his tribe warriors stepped back, for they had never seen any being like these. The angels said to King Trios, 'We are aware that evil has left you. We had to wait for this time, a time when your ancestor could be found and be released from his plight.'

"One angel approached Chief Amasis. He stood fearless. The angel said, 'Chief Amasis, as I speak to you, see the truth come alive. "You were taken from your mother's arms right after she gave birth to you by a selfish, greedy alien.'

"The alien was full of greed, hoping to use you as bait to receive riches from the queen, your mother.' "Although this is a lot of information to share with you, we do not have a lot of time. When touched, you will see and understand."

"Chief Amasis understood quickly, mostly because the kings

who sought him out through his vision showed him a lot. "Another angel said to Chief Amasis, 'You have a sword Moab gave you. It is yours from your mother's dimension. It was found with you when the thief left you on a planet far away from your universe. Only you can use the sword to release the king, for you have a good soul.'

"Chief Amasis proceeds onward to end the pain from the malevolent force that gripped King Trios. He touched the king with his sword. A magnetic, beautiful yellow highlight shone on him, and power flowed into the king's body.

"He got up, something he had not done for so long, and then the king broke his own chains. With the combined strength and courage of the tribes and the tribal aliens, they wiped out the evil ghosts that were there to fight.

"King Trios was freed from the darkness that previously ensnared him, feeling love and goodness once more. He acknowledged his guilt for neglecting his tribes. He quickly returned to them, hidden in the mountains, and returned all the alien tribes to their home planets in each of their dimensions, reuniting them with their long-waiting kin.

Chief Amasis had fulfilled his second call to his destiny. He immediately shut the chapter of debt owed by evil, releasing the hold on King Trios, and he scaled equal balance. Darkness was removed from Araila as well.

Dawn broke, and a golden hue of sunlight bathed the valley with the first rays of sunlight, revealing startling transformations of the valley and plains to a lush expanse of rolling hills and vibrant forests.

Chief Amasis and the tribes made their way to the cave after supporting Moab in the light of a new day. The winds were gentle. The rains cleared the air with a refreshing breeze, and renewal permeated the air. Moab and the aliens gazed out at a world reborn, a testament, resilience, and blessings bestowed upon them in the midst of the storms.

"As they prepared to leave the caves, by way of their destiny, Chief Amasis reflected on the journey they had undertaken. Of trials faced, alliances forged, and wisdom gained, which led them to this time and moment of triumph. They carried with them the knowledge that their destiny was intertwined with the very fabric of the universe, a reminder that even in the darkest of times, blessings could be found in the most unexpected places.

"And so, the tribes and the tribal aliens embarked on a new chapter, their spirits lifted by the victories of the past and the promise of a brighter future. Guided by the lessons learned in the depths of the mountain, they ventured forth with hope in their hearts and a determination to embrace the challenges that lay ahead, knowing that they carried the blessings of the storm with them, forever shaping their destinies.

"The birds were chirping, leading them to believe the cold season was ending. During winter, weather conditions were so harsh that birds could not survive if they entered the high atmosphere. Chief Amasis was pleased; he opened the large door to the cave. Walking out of the cave, he inhaled the air, lifted his arms to the heavens, and gave loud praise. The sky was clear, and as he looked into the valley, he could see the effect of the release of King Trios, and with a full heart from everything that happened below.

"Chief Amasis's tribes prepared to depart the cave that had

been home for a long time. There was an atmosphere of excitement in the air. The group never complained again about anything, knowing that they were saved and changed from their time in the cave by listening to Chief Amasis.

"They continued moving with intention on the trail of the mountain, enduring the last couple of weeks, resting in the open because the weather and atmosphere were incredibly perfect. Nighttime was the best, watching how the stars would line up and perform. They had never experienced seeing the universe like this before. The tribal aliens felt the stars were right on them while they slept at night. Not realizing that the stars were upon them.

"Chief Amasis felt moisture, the clouds got thick, and the birds dropped back below. He knew that they were getting closer to the top. He also notices the covering around them and the mountain."

Chapter Eleven

THE STORY: PART FOUR

The climbing stopped, and they began to walk on the side of a hill. It felt as though they were walking into an entrance that was covered and sealed above and behind them. Then, finally, they made it to the mountain top.

"They were all filled with happiness and joy. Chief Amasis was so elated, making it to the top of the mountain they so longed for. They remembered those they had left behind, feeling sorrow for those who remained and perished in the valley.

"Standing on top of the mountain seemed unreal. It was the hot season; the beauty of the landscape and tall buildings took their breath away.

The chief wondered who could have created something so magnificent as this place. It was so unbelievable that a little fear came into their hearts. Thinking that the alien race who lived here had to be powerful. All of the many different thoughts processed in Chief Amasis's mind, and he looked up and realized they were standing right in front of the building.

"Now, waiting to be greeted by those who gave them signs, got them out of the valley, protected them from the devastation, and fed them for months in the caves, they are not greeting them.

"This could have been a concern, but they had so much joy and happiness, and they believed that their life had changed forever. The tribe stood in front of the main building for hours. The chief was so relieved to be in a safe place that he respectfully decided it would not be a wise move to enter the buildings, so he instructed the tribes to set up camp outside. He knew whoever saved them would be back.

"As months passed, Chief Amasis and the tribal aliens enjoyed living without fear on the mountaintop. The mountain was so high the plains were invisible to the naked eye. The mountaintop was special. It was shielded by a thin cover, which protected them from the atmosphere of being so high in space.

They lived and enjoyed their newfound home in hopes that whoever lived on the mountaintop was harmless and good.

"The seasons began to change, showing many signs, as the wind blowing stronger and getting colder. The chief noticed the protection from the strong air and winds were diminishing. The weather changed quickly, and rain began to pour. The lightning was right upon them, and it was frightening. They could see into the sky and realize they were in space.

"The aliens had to hold onto each other and the structures to not be pulled into space. The stars were so close, almost touching. Then, suddenly, they saw large shadows falling down toward them. As these large aliens settled, they began to enter from the top of the building, flying down toward them.

"The chief thought about what he could do to save his tribes. They all wanted to run out of fear. The chief spoke to all of the tribes, saying, 'Hold still and face the objects flying fast into the mountain.'

One of the large figures landed with wings and stood in front of them. Their bodies were shiny and leathery because of the rain. The force from their presence and closing their wings brought high winds, which made the tribal aliens tremble. The aliens were wide and had wings hidden behind their tall forms, which carried fierce winds.

"As the aliens all entered the top of the mountain, a veil began to surround them again, and the winds softened as with the thunder. As the winds cleared, the rain also started to clear. The tribes and chief started to clear their faces and eyes and saw large forms. The chief did not know what to expect or say. He heard a strong, vibrating voice say, 'Do not be afraid. Welcome to our mountain of peace.'"

Chapter Twelve

REVELATIONS

After the warriors appeared, a very thin layer of invisible material above the mountain covered the tribal aliens again, and they were protected from the weather.

The tribal aliens are mesmerized, captured by the height and glow of the warriors. Chief Amasis felt familiar with the warriors and said, 'You have nothing to fear because I remember who the warriors are. They saved our lives.' The tribal leaders looked at Chief Amasis and asked, 'Are you okay? Because surely you could have never encountered these beings.'

"'Chief Amasis replied, I remember them". You were quite young when the evil aliens captured our community.' "'I was young but old enough to fight and escape the evil aliens. The warriors showed up and lifted me out of the evil alien's ship.' "'One of the evil aliens saw that I was carrying the sword from one of the elderly warriors". The sword was significant to the evil aliens because the sword carried an unknown power.

They understood taking me would be the key to defeating the warriors in the future. The evil aliens fought hard to take the sword and me away from the warriors but were unsuccessful.' "The warrior, standing in front of Chief Amasis, looked upon everyone and connected with each of the tribal aliens. The tribal aliens could feel the warrior communicating inside of them. All their fears dissolved and replaced with confidence and healing of the past.

The accumulated hurt from losing other tribal tribes in the valley and the hard life living there just passed, with a feeling of a light feather flowing from their heart, along with the original inhabitants' memories removed. "The warrior closed his wings, his body changed, and surprisingly, he looked more like them. As the warrior began to talk, everyone listened and got close. He explained how they watched out for Chief Amasis and the tribes during the mountain climb but could not interfere.

They waited for the tribes to make it to the top of the mountain, but the Realms opened for battle.

It was the Season of the Stars celebration in the universe, and the warriors left for battle. Before leaving, they safeguarded the tribes' safety and successful climb and secured a place for Chief Amasis from severe weather. Provisions were left in the caves to feed the tribes until they could climb again. "The warriors knew the Moab tribe and hoped they would be successful, fighting evil at all sides.

"They continued to embrace the chief and the tribes and revealed who they were, saying, 'We are warriors who lived in the universe for millions of years.' The warrior said, 'I am Aether, the leader of all warriors. We took this planet to save our alien race from a tragic loss of our planet, "opened the realm to this planet, needing a place to rest during battles in the universe. Telling the tribes about the purpose of their life, how they waited for the Season of the Stars that took place in the universe, and how they fought to protect all of the tribal aliens and stop evil from entering their planets in the galaxy.

"'We have missed our tribes, and now you are back after waiting years for you to come.' The warriors assured the chief and tribes that this was their home now. They would never live in the land of the Old-World descendants on the plains of the low valleys ever again.

"Everything and everyone left in the valley was destroyed and captured. The original inhabitants and the animals who terrorized the tribes were taken by their evil force. The twelve tribes who did not believe what Chief Amasis told them lost their lives because they were too afraid to leave. Their faith did not hold, nor did they remember that the chief was good. They forgot that 'Goodness is in the midst of power.' Chief had no fear, which was the reason they lived so long. The warrior continued to say, 'The tribes left in the valley were taken by the evil force, who travel through dimensions.'

"The alien tribes who would not come with Chief Amasis to the mountain top sealed their fate when they would not leave the valley. Aether, the warrior said the only way for everyone to be safe was to follow the agreement. In the agreement, they had to promise never to tell anyone about them, and they agreed.

"Years passed, and Chief Amasis helped the tribes to watch out for the warriors during the time of the battles. The tribal aliens called this time the Season of the Stars. This was an anointed time when strong thunder and lightning came from fighting in the universe, with the purpose of keeping evil from taking over the planets. This was a time of celebration, protection, and strength during certain times of the year.

"Many years passed, and the tribal aliens truly kept their word, and the warriors held theirs. The warriors spent longer lengths of time with the tribal aliens and gave them gifts. They became stronger, wiser, and lived longer.

"The children were born with special talents and grew to have a look like no other. They were brilliant, and all generations were born on the same date. Although they were born in different years, on the same date. These children carried a gene from the warriors with the ability to open the Realms to the universe.

"The children helped the warriors make their way through the loud thunder, lightning, and rain. They were born with a gift, and on their birthdays, the singing and celebration they made became a beautiful, serene sound that traveled throughout the realm and gave the warriors a clear pathway to the planet's realm. The sound was heard throughout the universe during battles.

"Throughout the many years and the many universal battles, time had become more dangerous. As the years passed, the tribes grew, and the children matured and ventured out to live in other places, showing their intelligence and strength to build homes that connected to the Aralia Realms, continuing the responsibility and promise to the warriors.

Their tribes grew, and families increased in the new land. They built communities and created traditions and celebrations that continued.

"As time passed, there were fewer with the full gene of the warriors. The tradition was in jeopardy. This could be a problem that could cause instabilities in the universe. Knowing this was going to happen one day, provisions were made secretly to ensure the Aralia realm would always be protected.

The gene predicted by the children of the warrior's centuries ago talked of an alien who would carry the gene and change the outcome of the wars that came into the universe. To give the warriors the power to control all the galaxies and bring peace to the universe again, forever.

End of the story…"

Tepa was so into the story that she moved to the floor to sit by her grandfather. She expressed to him how the story was the best she had heard. Grandfather smiled and said, "I hoped you would feel that way." Her grandfather looked at her and said, "I must tell you something."
He took her hand, lifting her up from the floor. He motioned for her to sit in his handsome, large, red chair. Tepa had always admired her grandfather's beautiful red leather chair; it was where he always sat.

Soon after the story, Tepa's mother and father came into the room. Tepa was glad to see them at first but became very uneasy and curious about why her parents showed up during her visit with her grandfather. She asked, "What is happening now? The story tonight was very overwhelming and made me feel that it was real."

Tepa began to think more about the story and showed frustrations, rubbing her forehead and almost filling her with tears in her eyes, saying, "There must be a serious conversation coming." Her grandfather said, "Tepa, listen to your parents." She quickly tried to calm herself down to listen. Her parents began telling Tepa things she did not want to hear. She said to them, "Not now, please." She was not ready and did not want her life to change.

Her parents, was at a loss, not understanding why she was so afraid, looked at her curl up on the couch in front of the fire. Her mother looked at her grandfather and said, "This is the young girl who was always the first to take a challenge." They sat around her and started to tell Tepa about all the stories shared with her throughout the years until now were stories about her ancestors.

Tepa responded, "It has become easier to believe anything right now." But she questioned, showing a smirky smile, "The flying warriors." Tepa always looking for a laugh from her family." The early evening turned into late night, while many considerable heartfelt conversations continued.

The family informed Tepa that it was time for training, as all generations had done. Tepa was told how important her role and life are for the tribal aliens. Training had to start now for Tepa, with some of the best in the universe.

They also told her that she would have added protection to make her feel secure with the changes to prevent obstacles. All the information had become overwhelming, and with even more for her to learn. Her mother and father shared how their family had been responsible for the survival of the Season of the Stars.

They told Tepa her genes were special, and she was chosen to change the outcome of the wars to come. Tepa's family hugged her, saying, "The training is for your protection."
But it was too much for her to take in, she asked, "Why can't I be protected here and train here?" As soon as Tepa asked, she realized, and quickly remembered, the secrets in the castle and then the book her grandfather had read to her earlier about her ancestors. Chief Amasis. Tepa wanted to do whatever she was asked; she was convinced.

She planned to learn everything she always wanted to know, mainly

who she was.

Chapter Thirteen

SEASON OF THE STARS

The mountains on planet Aralia were the most popular mountains for travelers. They visited all the mountains, except they were never allowed to go to the private mountains, villages, and towns, especially in the town called Crest Peak, which is located at a high altitude near the castle.

Five years had passed since Tepa was sent away for special training. The information she received five years ago regarding her life and every tribal alien's future on the planet of Aralia inspired her. This gave Tepa the purpose of living according to her destiny.

The history of her ancestors gave her a reason to be prepared and ready to answer her responsibility for what was to come. Now, she was back and carried a vastly different force around her. Although

Tepa did not see the change in herself; she realized others did.

Tepa's first stop was the library, her favorite place to explore daily as a young girl. She was wondering why the library felt different. In the past, she felt powerless and very humble. Now, she understood the privilege she felt was false.

Tepa's feeling of control and accessibility in the library had become a tool, and she knew how to use it.

Her parents and grandfather shared the knowledge of the Old-World planet Aralia. The tribal aliens also learned about the many sacrifices in their ancestors' lives for the goodness of the universe to overcome evil.

Every alien throughout the universe was aware and had been given power because of the understanding of what was at stake. Displays of notations of the tribal alien's tale were represented in the library.

Stories of power, obedience, and truth correspond with the trials and legacy of the ancestry tribal aliens, who traveled to the top of the mountain with Chief Amasis. All were written and revealed and would never be hidden again.

The written old documents gave more details of how grateful all the tribes were to the chief for his intuition to move the tribes out of the valley. Written documents from the tribes talked about how they looked down into the valley after leaving the cave and saw the great divide below the valley and how everything vanished into the abyss. The tribes who did not follow Chief Amasis perished.

The announcement was made to all the tribal leaders that this was the year a descendant of Chief Amasis, the leader who bravely led his tribes to the top of the mountain thousands of years ago, would start to take part in the Season of the Stars celebration.

Tepa and other special students were arriving for the Season of the Stars yearly celebration. The tribal leaders were excited to embrace the young adults as they took part in the celebration. The new generation of adults were taught from birth for this day. They were ready to participate in the tradition.

Tepa's thoughts were not about the things she had thought about as a young girl. She felt the pressure of making her parents and ancestors proud and described how she trained and prepared for the Season of the Stars celebration. How she waited patiently for the day to come she remembered the stories her grandfather shared which are now her reality.

Tepa was participating in something her parents and ancestors fought for, and she understood her duty to help protect her family, friends, and her world. Soon after the counsel's introduction, Tepa hurried into the celebration, where she saw her friends and family. She was slightly nervous and had so much energy building up inside she thought she would burst. It was the first time she saw everyone for years.

Tepa and others were all sent to a school far away in the mountains to learn the things their ancestors put in training for them. They all barely saw each other except for those who were her closest friends, like Eaton, one of Tepa's best friends. While away, Tepa grew into a beautiful young woman; it was hard for Eaton to think of her the way he did when they were younger. He watched as Tepa entered the room.

Training school gave Eaton a chance to see Tepa from time to time. The men were in one hall, and the women in another hall. Every chance he had to catch a glimpse of her made him happy. Eaton could not wait to see Tepa today. As she walked by him, she caught his eyes and gave him a beautiful smile. He could not keep his eyes off her. Eaton was determined to be cool and tried not to stare and smile so much at her. He did not want Tepa to know his true feelings.

Eaton's ancestors were a crucial part of the army, trained by Chief Amasis. He relied on them for years. As children, Tepa and Eaton always looked forward to taking part in the celebration called the Season of the Stars. She started to reminisce about the way they would hide under the staircase, listening to the excitement because they were never allowed to go to the top floor. The entrance was secure and locked until the adults were ready to come in or leave.

Tepa felt different as she entered the terrace landing of the castle, which was the highest place in the castle. In this area, the castle was extraordinary, with soaring ceilings so high that Tepa's bedroom window was in the clouds. The terrace floor of the castle was in Aralia's realm.

They were all entrenched in the celebration, with dancing and singing. The terrace was much larger than Tepa remembered. The columns stood tall, and each one was enormous, so much so that four of the largest tribal aliens could not stretch their arms around the columns.

During the earlier part of the night, Tepa observed a thin veil covering the terrace around the room of the celebration. She noticed a small opening at the very top corner of the veil, which meant the closure was not secure. Looking around for any of the elders, she could not find anyone who could help. She had no success in getting assistance.

Most of the new generation adults did not know that they were in an unseen bubble because the invisible material was so thin that it was as though nothing was there.

The night was amazing and beautiful. While the younger generations were examining how close the stars were above their heads, they were experiencing the sensation in their bodies. Stars pulsating and sending stimulating waves throughout the Season of the Stars celebration.

Sparks from the stars flowed into their bodies. They were shining so brightly that the light showed the passage from the top of the terrace to the inside of the Realms.

The young generations were captured by the astonishing sight of the universe as space covered the steps into the Realms as the steps disappeared into space.

Birds and other flying fowls, although exceptionally large, had left the terrace because of their ability to not survive in space. The species on the planet could not fly high and live. The celebration was great. Tepa and Eaton were having so much fun that they hoped it would last all night.

Tepa remembered in the past how the parents would be there all night and sometimes until the next night. They both laughed and said, no wonder they stayed so long having so much fun. They both were thinking so much of the past that they forgot about the crucial factors concerning the celebration. They were there for another reason.

The Season of the Stars celebration was an intricate piece of the reason for the season. As the evening continued, the celebration turned and began to unravel into something to be frightened of. The wind and fog moved onto the terrace floor, and the atmosphere changed quickly.

Once everyone noticed the changes at the celebration, they realized the Aralia's was completely open. Tepa knew something was not right, that the realm should not be open. Tepa said, "This is not acceptable and against all the rules of opening the realm."

She recalled seeing the opening earlier when she entered the celebration. Anxiety set in because Tepa felt responsible for not finding the elders. She was so excited about this day she forgot about the danger that lay beyond the Season of the Stars. She quickly looked around the room to search for her mother and father and could not find them, which caused her to panic, perceiving everyone was in trouble. The realm was open without the leaders knowing.

The foundation of the terrace built up an atmosphere that quickly changed. The veil had opened entirely, giving a pathway for the air from space to enter and flood the terrace. Everyone, plus Tepa's body, began to lift and feel lighter. She had no control and understood right away there was no gravity, as she was floating. All she could see was danger, especially for her friends. The adults who were experienced at this level of the Season of the Stars were not there.

Tepa looked out and found herself in the planet's realm. Freezing air was hitting her in the face, filling her lungs with moisture. The air caused the young adults to have a harsh time. The depleting of gravity caused them to lose control, while most of them found spaces to hold on to.

Reality

Tepa was pulled further away from the others. She was not able to control her direction. There was a stillness around her, and it felt like time was on hold. Tepa looked out and could see with bare eyes into dimensions in the universe. She remembered her time spent in the library, where she was pulled into space.

The beauty of the colors of blended arrays radiating from the stars encouraged her. Tepa passed through Aralia's realm and did not see anyone. She heard a voice faintly calling out to her. As the fog cleared, she saw her mother fighting and realized that her mother and father were in battle all this time with the warriors, prior to and throughout the Season of the Stars celebration.

Tepa believed something had gone wrong, and every move made had been controlled by a force. Warriors had been the keepers to the Season of the Stars for generations. They saw the tribal aliens were in trouble and entered the realm from battle to help. This was Tepa's first opportunity to observe a warrior. She had heard stories about them but had never seen them before.

The fighting was approaching her, and she noticed the warrior's long, magnificent body moving very swiftly, with open wings remaining focused like an arrow positioned at a target. The battle was why the realm was open and why her parents were not at the celebration; they were at war.

Earlier, before everyone arrived at the celebration, the counsel was called to duty. They left, knowing the new recruits would be alone. Tepa's mother saw the celebration starting and noticed the realm was also open. The leaders had spoken to the elders earlier, asking them to close the veil for protection and to watch out for the young generation during the celebration.

Now, seeing the realm still open, she knew it was too late to close it before everyone entered the celebration on the terrace of the castle. The elders knew that the new generation had not experienced this before and would not know that the realm was open. Someone let this happen purposely.

Her parents glared at each other. They knew this was bad and hoped they taught Tepa well enough to make it through it. Tepa's parents began moving toward the entry before the covering opened fully as the celebration was happening. They wanted to try and protect the young aliens before they were all pulled into the realm.

Her mother recognized it was too late to close the realm. She looked out and saw her daughter drifting within space. Tepa's mother's nightmare worsened as she attempted to get close to Tepa as she entered back into the realm, and was not successful and could not grab her. Her mother called out, and she turned to the sound of her mother's voice, but they could barely see each other because of the condensing fog.

After losing sight of Tepa in the mist of darkness, her father and mother knew she was in trouble. A battle was taking place, and Tepa was there in the realm, consumed in the battle. Her father and mother went back into the realm to help, but it was too late. Tepa was too far in the realm, and the warriors were unaware she was there.

Suddenly, a large dark image flew past Tepa. It was so close that the strength from its wind knocked her out. She was floating in the universe. Hours later, Tepa, found by the warriors and her father, who brought her back to the top of the terrace of the castle from the planet's realm found that no one was there, only the warrior who brought her back, and her father who laid her down softly. He left when he noticed his father, Tepa's grandfather, is coming far away. Tepa's father had to go back into the realm to find Tepa's mother. They quickly moved, believing she was absolutely in danger. Her mother lost control, distracted by seeing her daughter in the battle.

Tepa's father quickly left to find her before losing her to the evil aliens. The warrior and her father left; they saw Tepa's grandfather running to help her. Tepa's body was cold, and she looked as though she was asleep. Grandfather made an urgent call for the car to take Tepa to the refuge, a place of healing. Tepa's grandfather saw no signs of her parents. He understood his job was to take care of Tepa and then come back to find the rest of his family.

Chapter Fourteen

THE RESIDUAL

Two years passed, and Tepa finally opened her eyes. Her vision clouded and her mind foggy. Disoriented and struggling to comprehend her surroundings, wondering where I am and how did I get here? She recognized those tending to her, healers. She thought, why do I need healers?

The reasons remained vague. Tepa did not know she had awakened from a coma, a deep slumber lasting two years. They were surprised with her recovery, expressing joy at her ability to come through the coma. The healers asked her, "Do you remember anything about your injury?"

The only things she remembered were the dreams that tormented her while in the coma. She instinctively knew she must not divulge her dreams to them.

Before responding to the healers, a helper entered the room to tell of the imminent arrival of Tepa's grandfather.

When Tepa heard that her grandfather was coming, she felt anxious and pushed herself to remember, understanding that it was important. Her instincts were strong about her situation, and Tepa remained determined to recall the missing pieces.

Her thoughts were focused mentally and spiritually on searching for the fragments that would complete the puzzle. And then, it struck her. Some memories flooded back, pertaining to some of the actions taken that led to her injury.

Tepa's grandfather arrived, and he heard she did not remember what happened to cause her injury. He moved slowly as if he did not want to cause any noise. He was cautious. It was a habit from when she was in the coma.

Grandfather finally made it inside her room, and he gave Tepa a warm embrace. Delighted that she was awake, he heard she did not tell the doctors about how she got her injury. He was relieved. He felt assured he would finally have the answers to help find her parents.

The fact was that Tepa had not recovered all her memories, plus her parents were missing. When Tepa saw her grandfather, she looked for her mother or father. Tepa quickly understood and remembered enough to know something had happened to her parents.

Tepa's grandfather watched out for her in the coma and stayed day and night when he could. His faith kept him grounded, and he knew she would eventually wake from the deep sleep. Her grandfather understood the extent of her injury and what caused it.

Tepa could not wait. She reached and embraced her grandfather. She told him how, during her sleep, she felt his presence and grew closer to him. Although she was in a coma, she remembered him and waited for him to visit. The healers said other patients experienced the same feeling, having someone with them and hearing familiar voices from loved ones. The healers left the room to give her grandfather privacy. She anxiously embrace to her grandfather and communicating her concern about hearing her mother. Hearing her say, "Wake up and help her."

Tepa's grandfather explained to her that she still had a

connection to her mother and said, "We will get your mother and father back!"

Time passed quickly, and the healers asked Tepa about her parents. There was an understanding between the grandfather and Tepa to say her parents were traveling and would return soon. She felt pressured to remember everything that happened because she had the answers that could bring them back.

Tepa and her grandfather had to keep information about her parents' secret. They could not share it with anyone. No one would believe or understand what happened the night of the disappearance except for those of their tribes far from them.

Tepa was becoming an exceptional young woman, tasked with a responsibility to an alien tribal race. She believed it was important not to worry her grandfather about the dreams she had during her coma. She felt the dreams would go away, although they were getting worse. Tepa thought if she could remember everything that happened to her during the time her parents disappeared, she could free herself from her dreams.

After a year passed, Tepa's health and memory got better.

Grandfather knew that before he took her home, she had to finish training. He gave her a book that might feel familiar to her. It was in a leather cover with a relic art design. He hoped this book would begin the recovery process of Tepa's memory.

Tepa and her grandfather were not in the castle, which was their favorite place, in front of their large rock fireplace. Nevertheless, they resided at a gorgeous inn that had a large fireplace and, as usual, shared one of their favorite drinks. Her grandfather shared a book, hoping to inspire her memory.

He believed the book would bring about something great and would change her impending situation. He recalled the last book he had read to her, which really changed her life. He hoped this book would bring her strength and confidence to want to remember, without being afraid of what she experiences, and release her memory.

Tepa read day and night. She was quick and observant. Although she did not remember everything, she knew there was a connection to this book. Tepa was told that the stories were not made up but real-life experiences, like the books of her ancestors, which she did not remember. Reading the book gave her the impression of an instruction manual because it is truly her reality.

Tepa's grandfather reminded her of their home, where she had lived, learned, and loved for generations, hoping she would remember these connections in the book. As she read the book her grandfather gave her, it triggered feelings.

Tepa was concerned about her sleep because the dreams that started in her coma were becoming challenging, and she realized she lacked the experience to fight the visions. Tepa said, "I believe these dreams are real. Someone is trying to talk to me." Knowing it was not her parents, the cold, harsh voice gave her sudden fear and terrified her.

Tepa was concerned about going to sleep quickly. Her nightly horrid visions affected her. She fell asleep and was suddenly awakened by her own intense screaming. She was fighting something. Her grandfather heard her and ran into the room. He saw a figure flowing over her. It was clearly not in the room, as if it were trying to transport itself through Tepa.

He went to her bed quickly, grabbed her, and woke her. The

image disappeared, and Tepa opened her eyes. Her grandfather was so relieved he said, "This night is really unbelievable. Some actions need to be taken."

The next morning, Tepa awoke with her grandfather sleeping in a chair next to her bed. When she rose, she did not remember what had happened. Afterward, clearing her thoughts, she remembered and understood why he was there. She knew it was time to let him know what had been happening to her.

Tepa woke her grandfather with a cup of coffee and regretfully apologized for not telling him about her dreams. She immediately began to share with him about the struggle, how her dream was a nightmare. Her grandfather gave a heavy, distressed breath and responded, letting her know he was already questioning if she was touched by one of the evil aliens in Aralia's realm.

Especially after seeing her in her sleep last night, he saw what was hovering over her and how she was physically fighting it. Her grandfather understood what was happening and told her that someone must be helping her by keeping the image of her dreams blocked before it could capture her.

He was so thankful to know that she was saved and not lost like her mother and father. But because she was touched by the thing, it had a connection only while she slept.

Every night after the tragic revelation of evil attacking Tepa, her grandfather slept by her bed to guard against the enemy that was trying to enter the Realms through her. After weeks of offensive battles, Tepa's grandfather had to send for help from the Aralia realm. He hoped they would make it in time to save his granddaughter.

At night, they would play games and talk until the morning. The daylight kept the enemy away from her dreams. He felt time was running out, Tepa's grandfather saw that she looked extremely strong, and she was not worried. He thought, if she only knew the types of images she fought every night. Tepa asked her grandfather why she had so many bruises. She told him That she was not afraid and that she felt stronger than the thing that attacked her, although she felt that someone else was there helping.

During the evening, Tepa's grandfather stepped out of the room for a cup of tea for them both. He returned to her and found her in a state of shock. She was seizing. He could not get her to wake up. The image was able to knock him away from her body.

Tepa's grandfather was at a loss until he heard a loud knock at the door. He got up from the floor and ran to the door. He opened the door as quickly as possible, believing it was helpful there. He found himself on the floor again and did not know why. He got up from the floor and eagerly proceeded to Tepa's room.

He found her sitting up in bed with a man next to her. He could not see him clearly but knew he was someone good. He turned to Tepa's grandfather and said, "I am Chief Amasis." He smiled and said, "She will be fine now." He had a bag in his hand, tied with a gold string and a light inside it. He disappeared, leaving a trail of small stars sparkling behind. They were so tired and relieved they fell asleep.

The next morning, they woke up, although they remembered there were no discussions about what had happened the night before. Tepa's grandfather talked to the healers and said, "Tepa is healed and full of strength. We think it is time for her to leave." The healers agreed but sincerely cautioned Tepa, saying that leaving the place where she had spent a couple of years might cause her to feel uneasy at first. But all evidence pointed to a complete recovery. She would be fine.

Tepa was overwhelmed with anxiety, and a feeling of fear came over her. She understood the task ahead, wondering if she could fulfill her grandfather's expectations. Grandfather noticed Tepa's uneasiness, and he said, "Do not let concern consume your thoughts."

Tepa said, "Thank you for assuring me." Her grandfather said, "Time is closing in on us, and it is felt throughout the universe. Can you feel it? You have so much more to learn. And you are the key to getting your parents back. I feel taking you to the castle will give you the last healing." Tepa understood and agreed that he was right. She wanted and needed to be brave and strong.

They packed and left early in the morning because it was a long trip. Tepa had many thoughts while they traveled, such as how fascinating it was to ride the trains and meet her grandfather's friends.

They finally made it to the village. Tepa, totally exhausted from the travels, said, "I felt like we have traveled for days."
Her grandfather said, "You mean months." He smiled and said, "Where we are going, time blends automatically."

Tepa's grandfather reminded her that he brought her to the city when she got hurt to protect her. "And soon we will be arriving at the village, and I know you will love the village."

Time in the village was needed. Tepa enjoyed the sweet smells of the gorgeous flowers. She was not afraid of eating fruits hanging from trees, among bees, butterflies, and other insects. The colors and smells around the village were bursting with flavor. The buildings were tall, slender, small, and quaint, with sculptured designs of warriors. There were antique crosses sculptured throughout the town.

Tepa saw weeping willow trees, with the barks of the trees so thick and large it would take four grown aliens to wrap around the tree. Yet it was just as beautiful as everything else in the village. There were so many birds and beautiful colors of blue, red, white, and black. Large peacocks, she had never seen so many diverse types of birds in one place before.

Behind the village was a very wide and tall gate, which opened to the road that took her home. Tepa began to feel slightly depressed, not remembering the awesomeness of the village and everything she had seen that day. She questioned herself about how she could have forgotten such a beautiful life.

Grandfather motioned for Tepa to come to where he was. As she approached him, she saw the town and other tribal aliens. Tepa began to forget about her concerns and started having fun with everyone. They were enjoyable, and the festival was fun. It was so much food, more than Tepa could see. The tables were full of food, drinks, and dancing.

Women Tepa's age spoke, calling her by her name. Tepa believed she knew them. As the night went on and the dancing continued, Tepa loved every moment. She felt free and happy again. She was with the tribal aliens who knew her. Tepa asked, "What is the celebration for?"

One of the town inhabitants tribals said, "This celebrating is the beginning of the Season of the Stars.
" Tepa vaguely remembered something about the Season of the Stars and continued walking among the tribal families, meeting every alien in the town. Older alien inhabitants joined her as they were celebrating and dancing. They welcomed her into the dance.

One elder woman touched Tepa's head lovingly during the dance celebration. Her smell brought back a familiar feeling. She was dressed royally. Her clothes were beautiful, nice velvet clothing, with gold and gems around her neck and waist. There were also other women in bright decorative silk blends of clothing and jewels around their bodies.

Later, after an elder touched Tepa, she started to get dizzy. She said it felt like her eyes were covered by someone. With her eyes slowly closing without seeing who it was or being able to stop them, she eventually fainted.

Tepa slowly awakened in the midst of quietness above her, questioning if she was in a dream. Unexpectedly, her memories started to flood her mind, coming back to her like being pulled from deep, flooded water. Remembering emotional things like the very first festival when she was young. She could hear her mother's voice talking with everyone and playing with her as a young girl.

Actually, a lot of memories came back. She looked around and recognized her friends. Tepa's grandfather came to her to see if she was all right, and she told her grandfather everything that happened when she fainted. He was pleased with the memories. She shared everything.

Tepa was exhausted. Her grandfather noticed and said it was time to go home. He motions for the driver to come around. The car pulled up. Tepa and her grandfather got in the car and entered through the high iron gate toward a street filled with gems.

The car slowly moved and passed one of the elder tribal women, the one who touched Tepa. She gave a big smile and waved. Tepa asked about her, saying to her grandfather, "After the beautiful tribal woman touched me, I began to feel different." She shared with him the things she began to see about her life after being with her.

Tepa's grandfather told her that the woman was his sister. "Her name is Pipas, and she is one of the special women in our tribe, an Aralia Herald. You might not remember her because Pipas left home, and this is the first time I have seen her in a long time.

"When Pipas was young, she loved living in the castle. Our mother warned her to be careful when moving throughout the rooms, especially during my father's absence, as he was away a lot on missions. Pipas continued to do as she wished and learned the hard way about hidden places in the castle that could cause her harm. Not knowing everything about her life, she called her adventures scavenger hunts. She would not listen and, unfortunately, paid a big price.

"Pipas disappeared one day, causing our mother to go looking for her. She returned and found that our mother had left without anyone knowing it, and she never came back, nor could our father find her. Pipas never forgave herself for causing our mother to disappear looking for her.

"Pipas left our home and lived among the tribal communities, learning spiritual ways of healing, levels no one has ever reached. Our father heard later that Pipas had disappeared again, with no signs of her or where she would be. "Pipas finally returned after years, and she became an Aralia Herald, a type of assignment only given by angels and ambassadors.

She was chosen as the official messenger. When she arrives, it is a sign that something is about to happen. Pipas never felt the need to explain the changes in her life. There was power in her voice and confidence, and she was fearless after returning home."

Her grandfather continued to tell her how his father revealed to him that she could not share any information about the place she lived. They only know that she had a strong relationship with angels. "The women in our family are incredibly special to the universe. You have traits from a place that one day you may enter." As he talked to her about who his sister was, Tepa started to recall more things, and she told him how she remembered almost everything.

As they drove up the winding road, the air was fresh, and the land was beautiful. They passed many impressive huge and small homes with the type of architecture from their ancestors. Most homes in the community were built many years ago.

It was different living on Aralia Mountain, rather than every other place on Aralia. There was no place like dwelling there. Tepa realized how much she missed being home and was so glad to remember it. Finally, the driver said on the phone, "We are driving in the driveway." Although Tepa could not see anything, she saw the clouds and how they rested on top of the castle during the late evening. Grandfather smiled and said to her, "Welcome home, Tepa."

Arriving home was a great feeling. The castle was very welcoming and beautiful. Tepa became excited about getting out of the car, and she was glad to be home. Looking up at the castle, Tepa remembered how the upper part of the castle was covered by clouds. She took a deep breath and smiled at the beauty of the castle. As she slowly exhaled, her thoughts were filled with how a magnificent structure like this was built by her ancestors. Believing she was part of her ancestors' lives, more now than ever.

The great Aralia castle was said to have been built by ancestors, angels, and warriors and sat on the highest mountaintop in the community. While looking out the windows, in any room of the castle, you could see a panoramic view that opened, seeing the community.

Higher in the castle, in other rooms, there was another surprise, glimpsing clouds. But cloudless moments in the rooms showed beautiful scenes among valleys, streams, and magnificent sparkling gems among the streets in the city.

When Tepa got to her room, she was so tired. She had just enough strength to open the window, and the cool breeze from outside increased her energy.

Tepa was mesmerized by the feeling of the air and the enormous birds sitting on the edges of the window. As the seasons began to change, the clouds appeared to be thicker outside. They were so thick you would think you could walk right out the window on them.

Although the castle was cold, she had a warm feeling of love and thought how good it was to be home. Tepa smiled and looked to be greeted by the staff who basically took care of her most of her life, but they were not there. She saw no familiar faces; the staff had changed. Her grandfather hired unfamiliar staff and explained how the old staff did not want to stay when he left to take care of her.

The staff complained that the castle was altering and could hear voices coming from the corridor. Each time they would check, no one was there. The voices continued and one day stopped, but the loud noises, knocks, storms, and other sounds continued as if the images and visions of the ancestors were alive and wanted to come out.

Grandfather told Tepa he wanted to bring them back, but he was not sure who was trustworthy since they did not know who caused the tragic accident that happened three years ago.

Tepa was in her room, quietly recalling how she enjoyed spending time throughout her chambers. She could see the Realms on one side of her sitting rooms, mostly during the freezing rain that would outline the Realms' design. In the larger private space, the windows were the only protection from the outside. There were no walls.

Here was where Tepa witnessed some parts of the adult celebrations, which lasted into the late hours of the night when she was young. Parents would bring their children to stay the night. Tepa remembered that they had the greatest alien sitter from another planet, and all the kids loved her. They played games and had tricks, and the children had fun, especially Tepa, since it was at her home.

Her family hosted important gatherings and festivities; it was the way of life living in the castle, and it was especially important to her parents. Tepa understood why it was so important now more than before. The children would leave early the next morning; sometimes, before Tepa woke, she would barely make it to the door or window downstairs to wave while their parents drove out of the driveway.

Tepa's curiosity remained the same, but she was more focused because of her experience during the last couple of years. She still wondered and was concerned about why the evil aliens hated her. At least she understood where her parents and the other parents went during the night. She always prayed for their safety.

Watching her mother during breakfast the next morning after the celebration indirectly changed the subject when asked about the parents' party. Tepa remembered her saying to her, "How was the night with the babysitter and the other children?" She also asked if she enjoyed the birthday party. Tepa always replied, "Yes, we love her, and she remembers to do all the fun celebrating birthday things."

Everyone in the community's birth date was during the Season of the Stars. The adults celebrated their birthdays at night on top of the landing. Tepa remembered the late-night sounds, feeling the vibrations in her room, and always wanted to go to the top-floor landing for her birthday.

During the Season of the Stars, which was an extremely dangerous and important night, there was a thin covering on the top-floor landing that protected everyone from seeing into the Aralia realm. Over the years, Tepa came to realize how dangerous it was for her father and mother.

She thought back and hoped she listened well enough and learned enough to be ready for anything that could happen. Since her parents and grandfather sent her to training, Tepa remembered how her parents and grandfather told her they had something to share with her.

That night, she found out who she and her ancestors were and received power in the knowledge of her legacy. Tepa understood the reality of the expectations in her life. She now understood the power she had inherited, which she carried through great family knowledge and influence, which changed her life forever.

In the meantime, grandfather searched for Tepa to share another book, which seemed almost identical to the other two books but they are different. It had a beautiful red leather cover. Tepa immediately opened the book, but not before admiring the beautiful red leather cover. As she read, she remembered more of her life in the castle and the feeling she had the night her parents disappeared.

"The Book of Warriors." It taught how warriors gathered within the Season of the Stars and were welcomed by one who had a gift to see into the Aralia realm. This person was born during the Season of the Stars and understood and accepted the purpose of being called on to open the Aralia realm and provide a safe place for the warriors during battles in the Season of the Stars.

The aliens were called Aralia warriors, who supported the battle, which could never be lost because if ever lost, it would be the end of Aralia as they knew it. "In the Aralia realm, warriors are larger than giants, holy beings; their bodies transcend and are divine, and their strength is felt before you see them.

They are assorted in many colors, and at times, they are all the same color. The warrior's purpose leads to the Aralia realm to bind the dominions, powers, and rulers of the darkness in the universe, cast down wickedness in high places, and render them harmless and ineffective against the high good power of all aliens.

"Aralia is a special planet. It is hidden and protected by a family of generations, who are chosen by the time of their birth and understand their purpose." As Tepa read the Book of Warriors, she felt bad, thinking that she was not ready to participate in the Season of the Stars birthday celebration, and she felt that her actions had caused the tragic act to happen during their birthday celebration.

Tears running down her face, she blamed herself, saying, "This was my calling, and I did not take it seriously enough and lost my parents in the realm." Tepa needed guidance and prayed to ask God for understanding and bravery to learn everything she needed to know to bring her parents back.

Tepa remembered the past, how she and her friends found themselves on the tenth floor below the landing of the Aralia realm. They escaped Nan, the sitter, and left their birthday celebration, determined to celebrate with the adults.

The adults did not know they had spectators. Tepa, along with the other children, were singing and dancing. They felt independent, dancing and enjoying each other. The teenagers suddenly felt mysteriously powerless and found themselves suspended in the air. They were underneath the landing, covered by a grid that protected them from floating. The atmosphere changed, causing weightiness, and the dancing of the teenagers came to a halt.

The younger aliens followed Tepa and the others to the party. They did not understand what they were doing; they were just following the teenagers and entering when the realm opened. They could not go back because there was no time to think. Tepa saw the children quickly snatched up to the landing. When the parents noticed them, it was too late to capture them.

The parents were saddened to see the children go into the Aralia realm; it was open, and a battle was taking place outside the realm.

Suddenly, hard rain and wind were blowing fiercely; Tepa was unsure if this was normal for the celebration because the rain and wind were causing the thin line between the Realms to vanish.

Tepa screamed to the rest of the young aliens to hold hands and prepare for the severe thunderstorms. She told them the Aralia realm must be open and that they should stay quiet so no one could see them. No one knew they were here, and right as she finished consoling her friends, a figure attempted to grab Tepa through the grid but could not get through. It would not stop until a large, beautiful being showed up, and then the figure left immediately.

Tepa could not explain what or who she had seen. She had forgotten this experience and could remember now that her memory came back. She was recalling things she had hidden out of fear, though the experience was a dream since nothing like this could be real. The winds were strong, and Tepa saw a world that existed that she could not believe. She was stunned and fainted. Tepa thought joy, love, singing, and dancing would be the greatest experience until the grief from the young alien children was taken by something never seen before.

The next day, no one talked about the celebration. The secret had revealed itself, and the stories her parents told her about the

opening of the Aralia realm were more than they said. When the

following year came, Tepa had a better understanding of the

Celebration of the Season of the Stars. She decided it was safer to wait

for her parents and others to introduce them to the world of the Season

of the Stars celebration.

Chapter Fifteen

REMEMBER EVERYTHING

Tepa's heart raced as she searched for her grandfather, so very eager to share with him the memories that flooded back from the events of three years ago. The Season of the Stars celebration held the key to understanding what truly happened that evening.

Tepa was determined to provide her grandfather with the answers he had long sought. Before she found him, Tepa was filled with hope and urgency, preparing her voice to reveal answers to so many questions about what happened at the celebration.

Her grandfather never got a chance to understand what happened at the Season of the Stars celebration because he was not there until the end of what happened with his family.

The information in Tepa's memories could finally be helpful and give him precise answers to what he believed happened. Tepa, unfolding the joyous atmosphere in the celebration, said, "The laughter created a kind of joy that turned gradually into something dark." Tepa vividly described how gravity itself failed, causing her to float helplessly into the mysterious realm.

Tepa tried but could not get control of her body, and it was useless. She said, "The Aralia realm was left open, which was the cause of everything happening the way it did during the celebration." She explained, "When I walked onto the landing, I felt moisture in the air and saw a corner open in the veil. Feeling that it was not normal, I looked for someone to tell. There was no one from the council around to give help."

Tepa confided in her grandfather, asserting that someone was responsible for this breach, and they had to be held accountable for the losses suffered by their community.

Her grandfather's anger surged as he realized the danger his granddaughter had faced, causing his protective instincts to flare up. Tepa continued to describe the evil radiating from the towering figure she encountered, how it sought to invade her mind, probing and tainting her thoughts.

Fear gripped her as she struggled to hide, realizing the figure's relentless pursuit of her. It became chillingly clear that the creature harbored an intense hatred, fixated only on her. Her only thoughts were of escaping back to her parents.

Tepa's grandfather patiently listened to her account of what happened three years ago and also felt responsible for the families at the celebration.

Tepa's grandfather had traveled over the years, training and selecting aliens known to have integrity, honesty, and loyalty. Knowing someone allowed a towering figure to roam around in the realm and affix its eyes on not only his granddaughter but also Aralia's future really angered him.

Tepa was frightened and attempted to hide from the evil alien who rushed at her. It focused on her as though his purpose were to capture her. Tepa knew she was in trouble because the figure wanted her and only her. It was extremely creepy. All she could think of was to make it back through the realm on top of the landing.

Tepa mother had taught her about the vulnerabilities of alien minds. She warned her of evil aliens who had penetrated the minds of innocent tribal aliens, influencing unsuspecting victims, silently seizing control of them. Amid the chaos of battle, with thunderous clashes and crackling lightning filling the galaxy, Tepa watched as the warriors valiantly fought against the malevolent forces.

Still, they were oblivious to her trouble, unaware of the looming danger Tepa faced. Her mother's eyes transformed into darkness. It was a telltale signal that she had succumbed to the enemy's influence.

Desperate to save her mother and draw the warriors' attention, Tepa screamed so hard, piercing the evil alien's mind, causing unpleasant pain before the merging of spiritual channels in battle. Afterward, the warriors finally heard Tepa's screams and immediately rushed to her aid.

However, their noble intentions were thwarted by the relentless assault coming from evil aliens. Tepa lost sight of her mother when they struck her. Through her fearful recollection, she said, "I never imagined not ever seeing my mother again."

Her father, full of guilt, hurried to escort Tepa into the realm's entrance, promising to find Tepa's mother and rescue her from the clutches of their enemies.

Tepa's determination to help her father in his quest led her back into the Aralia realm. When she approached space outside the Realms, it was disheartening. Her mother had endured a frightening change, and as Tepa struggled to follow her father's path, a colossal figure struck her, hurling her into the abyss of the galaxy.

The vigilant warriors managed to rescue her just in time. They returned her back into her father's open hands. He said, "Tepa, what did you do?" and laid her gently on the landing, where she slipped into a coma. Her grandfather was close enough to see Tepa was in trouble and understood what he needed to do for her. His son trusted him to take care of her.

Tepa was trying to remember more, and her grandfather saw that she needed rest. He said, "Tepa, you have to relax." She said to him, "Let me finish with my account of what happened."

She told him, "After she was struck by the figure holding her mother, she felt that something was about to happen, she told him that she followed her father back to the Aralia realm. She saw the control this figure had over her mother.

Tepa looked seriously at her grandfather, eyes filled with unknown answers and secrets unseen nor heard. She asked, "What are we going to do?" The information Tepa shared helped him understand more about the 'type of evil aliens' who might have his family.

Grandfather said, "Tepa, God will show me how to get them back, but now you have a great responsibility to Aralia and the communities to be ready to lead one day."
She replied, "Yes, I understand more now than ever the importance of staying safe and securing myself so I can finish training." Tepa prepared for her travels.

Time had passed. Tepa was still enrolled in the institution of Paramilitary Training, an environment of learning extremely advanced thought transference and theories, building strength constraints during warfare. She embraced the rigorous culture of education and competition, among others, while carrying positive attitudes that were encouraged by her unwavering dedication to family legacy.

Tepa developed exceptional intelligence and rapid learning abilities, which showed in her growth and maturity. Her mind remained steadfast and focused on her loved ones.

She recognized this training was essential for Aralia's future leadership, and she pursued it with unwavering determination. Being fully immersed in studies, Tepa remained aloof from social interactions, but her colleagues viewed her as a natural leader, treating her with respect and admiration. Professors recognized her potential, often entrusting her to help other students with trials and tests.

Tepa occasionally speculated about her own life, striving to be positive and keeping her ancestral responsibilities at the forefront of her mind. One day, Tepa hurried from her fighting class and noticed a fellow student who was constantly present wherever she went. Intrigued yet cautious, she observed his persistent smile and unwavering attention. Despite finding him attractive, Tepa made it clear through her gaze that she desired distance. Confused by his continued presence despite her disinterest, she could not fathom why he would persist.

Tepa reached home, changed hastily, and made her way to a special project requested by her professor. The opportunity filled her with both excitement and anxiety. After entering the tall building, she started to recall the attack that had happened at the castle years ago.

She consoled herself, saying the castle's height stood higher than the building she was entering and any other structure on the planet, which assured her that no harm should transpire.

The rooftop of this building was higher than other campus buildings; classmates were already assembled and waiting for Tepa's arrival. The professor expressed relief seeing Tepa's timely appearance.

She was teaching a class that would bring an understanding of the works and the interconnections of universal travel throughout the Aralia Realms. The professor acknowledged Tepa's exceptional knowledge. He entrusted her with instructing students about the realm's intricate mechanisms and the vital task of safeguarding the planets.

Tepa shared her knowledge about the Realms in the universe, knowing that more of her classmates would not have the privilege of knowing what went into keeping the planets safe. Continuing to delve deeper into explanations, the students were intrigued by their propounding understanding.

She almost lost her focus for a minute and began to be concerned about the strength of the structure. She questioned if the building was strong.

The winds quickly increased and created whistling sounds, turning into a disturbing storm and unleashing fury. Lightning cracked loudly across the sky; the thunder was echoing fiercely. Tepa heard a sound far off. She moved to an area away from the students who were very anxious. She felt something was wrong, and she did not want anyone around to get hurt. She heard many eerie sounds and distant voices, voices she could not tune out.

Instinctively, she stayed away from the others, even as

the professor instructed everyone to retreat to the lobby for safety. Alone on the rooftop, Tepa knew she had to face whatever was happening on her own. Feeling a deep passion to sing, she tilted her body and began to sing. Her voice joined the tempestuous symphony around her. She could see the realm opening and heard voices, and she recognized her mother's voice.

Her eyes widen, full of complete astonishment at the sight of her mother's appearance, saying to Tepa, "Return home to your grandfather." She assured her to remember, you know how to find us." The presence of others was with her mother.

Tepa was not afraid with her newfound confidence, which kept her strong. The realm closed, leaving a profound relief knowing her mother was still alive. However, danger was not far behind. The raging winds threatened to overwhelm her until someone materialized and guided her to safety inside the building.

Tepa looked into the face of her persistent classmate, realizing it was the same person who had been following her. His voice filled with reassurance, imploring her not to be afraid, and he asked, "How did you forget me?"

Tepa was startled by his question and asked, "Who are you?" He introduced himself as Eaton, her friend from Aralia. Memories flooded her mind; she felt like the ocean had let her flow up from the waters, and Tepa was moved to tears. "After years of events and trials, she had forgotten him," she explained.

Tepa was more than grateful to have Eaton back, thinking she had lost everyone from her past. She immediately started to smile again, showing all her beauty. They sought shelter together and engaged in heartfelt conversations never shared before.

"How could I forget you?" she said.

He said he heard her mother on top of the high-rise building, not only her mother but his family also. Eaton and Tepa talked about everything. Tepa detailed her life after seeing him last at the Season of the Stars. They listened to each other attentively.

Finally, exhaustion claimed both of them, and they drifted off to sleep, comforted by the sound of rain outside.

Tepa, sound asleep, was woken by a jolt of strong anxiety coursing throughout her. She confided in Eaton, recalling her experience on the rooftop of hearing her mother's voice and explaining to him that her presence was real.

"Eaton, she instructed me to help my grandfather and told me to find him. How can he be lost and or need help? He would have called me." Tepa planned her return to the castle immediately to see if her grandfather needed her help from grave danger.

Chapter Sixteen

THE RETURN TO THE CASTLE

Returning home brought Tepa face-to-face with reality. She opened the front door and swiftly moved throughout the castle into every room, looking for her grandfather. She found no evidence of him, and she became concerned. Eaton tried to support Tepa, reminding her to stay in faith and remember that her grandfather was a smart and brave leader.

She gathered the staff to talk about her grandfather's disappearance. All the staff that came were unfamiliar and made her uncomfortable. There was no trust among this group because they were not around when Tepa was growing up.

There was one person who spoke for all the staff in the residence. He asked Tepa to call him Aether. He had a warm smile, which helped Tepa to relax. Aether told Tepa that her grandfather was here more than he had been in the past, and he spent most days in the library and his office. Sharing how her grandfather believed he could bring Tepa's parents back home. Aether said he asked for his help.

Tepa asked, "Why would he need your help? You cannot know our family or our history." Aether walked closer to her and Eaton, looking into Tepa's eyes, and said very cautiously, "I know everything about our family."

Listening to Aether's response surprised Tepa. She thought she heard him wrong. Tepa asked him again to repeat what he had said. Hearing what he said again gave her pause and confusion about everything she knew about her family.

Tepa asked, "Are you family? And if so, where have you been?" His reply did not help much, for he moved on to say, "We need to find your grandfather, which is the most important thing right now." Tepa agreed with him, bringing her thoughts back to what was more important.

Tepa just did not know what to do. She thought of Pipas, her aunt, the only family she knew her grandfather had. She immediately began to recall conversations between her and her grandfather. Especially the conversations she thought were not important. Although Grandfather's sister was not around her growing up. Tepa knew finding her would help find answers. She mostly answered about incidents she might not remember over the years, such as her childhood as a young girl.

Tepa traveled to the tribal community to look for Pipas, and she remembered what her grandfather said: "She resides with the tribal community." She had to find her and tell her that her grandfather was missing. She got to the tribal community, but Pipas was not there, and no one could give her any information. A tribal sister heard Tepa ask for Pipas and began to call out to Tepa and motioned for her to follow. She went into a building, and Tepa walked in after her. She felt something different from what the community portrayed when she was there before.

Pipas left a package for Tepa and told her tribal sister to give it to her when she came looking for her. Pipas knew that Tepa would come to find her when she found her grandfather was missing. In the package was a unique metal box wrapped in material that she recognized, like Pipa's silk, in many colors and types of clothing. She was given many things in the box, such as a journal that stood out to her.

It was the key to hopefully finding some answers. Reading her grandfather's sister's journal, she found a heading with the words, 'the secret passage in the library.' Tepa continued to read the journal, looking for any information that could help find her grandfather.

Pipa and her father

Pipa wrote how she found a passage to enter the universe, which materialized when she followed her father into the place where he was working. Connected to the universe of beings, Pipa's father also traveled among the angelic aliens. The interstellar center he created was important to the ancestors. He believed that if he placed the center behind the library, the location would be undetectable, keeping it from being found and sabotaged.

The stair chambers would move aliens throughout dimensions without entering planet Realms. Pipas had no idea what she was witnessing. How important special aliens were in another dimension.

Her father lived for many years. No one could actually say what his age was. He knew unbelievable stories about the 'Great Twelve Kings' of the universe. It hurt him to see the end of an era of magical times in the universe.

He attended the last Season of the Stars with the young King Odonias as a fellow alien sharing the genes chosen by the angels. When he returned, he was more in control of building the center to transport aliens from the new universe to connect with the child who would be born with a special gene.

Pipas became jealous of the aliens, not recognizing that she was special. It was very disappointing for a young Pipas. Pipas wanted to show her father that she was as special as the alien with the special gene, so being in places she should not have caused ongoing risk for herself and others close to her.

Following the middle stairs in the interstellar center, she found herself in a bubble filled with air carrying her into space, happening without her control. Pipas tried to call out but could not be heard. She was lost, but she survived by a group of angelic aliens who enclosed her and moved her into another universe.

The way the interstellar room was supposed to work. Pipas traveled through a cloud, with shimmering radiant lights inside the clouds. She was taken to a room where a DNA test was given to Pipas to see why she could move up and down the stairway. Pipas's father was traveling and unaware of her situation.

She was lost, and no one could find where she was. The aliens from the new universe discovered through tests how Pipas was gifted and required training. Pipas wrote that they kept her for years and sent her back to wait to report to them when the day of reckoning was at hand.

"Tepa, I have left to inform them of the signs that have taken place."

Pipas wrote in a letter to her, saying, "Tepa, it is your destiny to now go forward and take your place. If you are as intelligent as I believe you to be, find your grandfather, use your gifts."

Tepa Overload

Tepa returned from seeing Pipas, saying, "She had left." But not before leaving her a letter and her personal journal. Aether knew to watch out for Tepa because the information did more than she realized. Receiving an overload from the communication from Pipas released her hidden memories so she could remember how to help find her grandfather.

Tepa fainted. Recalling things so quickly and overcrowded her thoughts. Both Eaton and Aether caught her before hitting the floor and placed her on her grandfather's large red chair in front of the fireplace.

Tepa woke and found herself sitting in her grandfather's large red chair, which caused tears to roll from her eyes. She missed him. Eaton was on one side, and Aether was on the other side. Holding her hands, Eaton questioned her, "Are you all, right? What happened?" Without answering the questions, Tepa looked up at Aether and said, "It is you! Right?" He replied, "Yes, Tepa, it is me."

Tepa believed that her visit during the time spent in Pipas's beautiful tent of sweet aromas and exotic figurines opened her senses to the true message. To remember when she was young, how she found the hidden entrance after trespassing the "Do Not Enter" sign. How she found the four stairways, and now realizing she was never by herself in the passageway. Tepa remembered more about her experience of meeting Aether and other things that happened in the secret place when she was a young girl.

The hidden room was a secret that Tepa did not think about again. She remembered how she passed through the library and found the four stairways. She walked up the stairway into a corridor and saw a glass door, opened it, entered, and saw the most beautiful vision she had ever seen. The ambiance of it all occupied Tepa so that she allowed herself to be pulled into deeper space. She was in a bad predicament and thought she caught herself floating in the air.

There were times in the Aralia realm when Tepa fought to get away from an alien. Now she realized why the alien continuously attacked her even in her coma. It knew her. She was thankful for the warrior who came to her bedside during her healing from the coma and again from being taken by the alien.

The warrior who helped her was family, and now she remembered how he helped her during past times in her life. Tepa nervously could not understand why her memory of the time spent outside the glass door had been forgotten.

Aether told her that the warrior wanted her safe and knew that the only way would be to remove your memory of the entire experience from outside the opening of the stairway.

Tepa returned home. Everyone was in town for a three-day festival, and they believed Tepa was with her parents. She never knew she was away for a long length of time. Tepa finally realized what these encounters meant; she had come full circle, knowing the purpose of all of the evil alien attacks.

Tepa felt a power inside her, and she accepted the responsibility to fight for Aralia's destiny. She thought back on that young, bold girl who knew she was something special. Tepa understood that only she could find her family and that she had always been the key. She would do whatever it took to bring all of the tribes together again. It was her destiny.

Tepa immediately started searching her grandfather's office to see if he had left any clues as to what happened to him. She found a case in an old antique desk with an odd lock on it, one she had not seen before. The case had a handprint underneath it. Puzzled by the odd lock, Tepa attempted to open the case with no success.

Aether studied the case; he knew what it would take to open it. The case was locked with a precision handprint, made to fit one person's hand. If the person who touched the handprint was not the exact fit, the safety protocol would cause harm to whoever tried to open it.

Tepa knew the case had information in it that would answer questions about her family and hopefully help find her grandfather. Her attitude toward the situation of her getting hurt from not being the person with the right handprint was a chance she had to take. Tepa was going to place her hand on the case. She believed in her destiny.

Although Tepa felt sick in the pit of her stomach. She believed the lock would open when her handprint was on it. Eaton noticed her nervousness and placed his hand over hers. They both relaxed their hands on the handprint. It lit up, pulsating beautiful colors, and the case opened.

Inside was a stiff red leather book that looked like it had been encased for many years. When the book opened, something happened to her. She screamed that her bones were on fire. No one could see anything wrong with her. She continued to scream what she felt; electricity was in her body.

Tepa fell out and got quiet while holding onto the book. When she woke up and rose to look at everyone to tell them that she was okay, both Eaton and Aether looked at her with concern. Tepa's eyes were golden, and her hair started to change as they were looking at her aura, golden like glistening water.

Aether got closer to the book and saw that it was the book many had searched for over many years. "The Book of Angels," a book that generations talked about, but it was never found. The book explained how angels gathered within the universe to open the realm during the Season of the Stars.

The book also explained that warriors were special beings, like angels, who protected and controlled all the planets' Realms in the universe. The warriors were highly skilled in fighting and subduing anything that tried to spread evil or harm in the universe. They opened the Realms and provided a safe place for planets in the universe to live away from evil.

As "the Season of the Stars" opened, there was another group of alien races who were responsible for each planet. On Aralia planet, they were called the "Aralia Heralds." Their purpose was to support the battle of good and evil. They used the skills they had developed over generations to create powerful singing voices to calm the Realms.

Without the Heralds, all the planets would be at risk.

It was written in the Book of Angels that a great power would be given to an Aralia inhabitant, which would change all the Realms in the universe to be controlled by one who would be more powerful and greater than the warriors and the Heralds of ancestors, who always supported the battle to conquer evil.

Chapter Seventeen

ANGELS CONQUER

In the spirit realm, angels were larger than giants, holy beings. Their bodies transcended divineness, their strength was felt before they were seen, and they were luminous yet all the same color. An angel's purpose in the spirit realm was to bind the evil principalities and subdue their powers.

The angels had the power to break the bonds of the evil rulers of the darkness in the universe and to tear down spiritual wickedness in places unknown, rendering evil harmless and ineffective against the children of God, every alien and being.

This special place on Aralia was hidden and protected by a family of generations who were chosen at the time of their birth and who understood their purpose.

Tepa remembered her ancestors as alien beings from the books she read. She understood that there was a chosen person who carried the special gene to change the outcome of the wars to come.

It was also written that warriors would control all the galaxies and bring peace to the universe again.

"I can now accept that this alien is me, especially since my hand opened the case to the Book of Angels, a case that only the descendant of warriors and angels could open," said Tepa.

Aether told Tepa and Eaton a story of how evil aliens and warriors were of the same ancestry. "They were impressive kings who became jealous of a special young king who was a spiritual being; they were all living in the universe together, and each had responsibilities for their own planets.

Seeking power and riches changed their hearts, leaving them with a jealous spirit, which opened the door of evil into the universe, allowing evil to enter from a deep, three-dimensional black hole.

"The kings never considered how their actions would interfere with the planets they ruled or lose their hearts to be taken over by evil aliens.

"The evil aliens grew in numbers and tried to take over the galaxy. The kings who were warriors were removed and transplanted deep into the universe. They were not considered as warriors anymore. The evil kings carried an appearance of hate and darkness in their eyes. The cold and wickedness in their spirit was felt within the warriors," Aether spoke as if he was there. They are evil and do not care about life.

As Tepa listened to the story that Aether was sharing with them, she suddenly remembered her mother's message. She explained the message her mother had given her to Aether.

She said, "'Come and find me,' while I was on top of a high building with students at a professor's event. My mother said, 'You know how to help us, just remember.'"
She thought to herself for a moment, and her face suddenly lit up like a light beaming, and she realized it could only be this place. She left Eaton and Aether, saying to them, "Follow me. I know where to go." She ran through the library halls until she finally saw the sign still standing like the day she ignored it. Seeing it again was surreal.

Feeling disturbed with guilt, she moved as quickly as she could, trying to block out hearing repeatedly that everyone told her to remember, now concerned that she had not figured out this key place sooner. Passing the "Do Not Enter Sign," she hurried through the door, hoping it would open, and then into the non-elevator, removing the hidden camouflage.

In the meantime, Aether understood where she was going. Eaton was in awe of the amazing technology. Tepa found herself facing the four-way stairway with Eaton and Aether following her. Eaton told Tepa to slow down and tell him what she remembered. Tepa responded to Eaton, "It is too much to explain now."

She ran up the stairway into the corridor, where all of the stairways meet. She inhaled and said, "Finally. I see it was not a dream." She found herself in front of the glass door. She looked at Eaton and Aether and told them that she believed her grandfather went through this door, and she must go through the door to bring him and her parents back.

Tepa said to Eaton, "I need you to listen to what I have to tell you. It is important." Struggling to speak without losing her mind, she had to tell Eaton what she learned years ago. Filled with anticipation, she revealed,

"There is a hole in space, a place where the evil aliens live. They have captured many tribal kings and other aliens, holding them for years, waiting to use them as a trap to capture the last alien with the warrior's genes.

"They captured me years ago, wanting to hold me there until an ancestor rescued me. The evil aliens have wanted me and my entire family for a long time. All of our ancestors are powerful, and as a group, we have the power to close the hole in space and send the evil aliens away for good. Which is why the aliens have been trying to take me hostage."

"The evil aliens were not successful in taking me through the hidden place where they are from, and I know our lost families are there. Aether and I have to save them."

Eaton was in disbelief and said, "Why would you decide to do this? You are finally back in my life, Tepa. I am totally against this idea." Eaton felt he had to go and protect her.

Tepa hugged Eaton and cried, "It is taking all my strength not to stay with you. We have to think about our responsibility to the universe, which is greater than ourselves."

Tepa convinced Eaton that every step taken was destined for all good. She said to Eaton if something happened to her and her family, he was the only one left to lead the tribal community.

Aether told Tepa it was time; he did not want them to be detected by any evil aliens. When she touched the door, it automatically opened. Tepa was shocked when she realized the door was thick ice, something she had not noticed before.

Tepa and Aether passed through the thick ice door into a tunnel. They were suddenly pulled into the hull of a spaceship. There was silence until light entered the opening of the hull. As the hull opened more, Tepa could see out into the universe.

For a strange reason, she knew that she was safe; Tepa was not afraid of the shadows in their mist. The figures begin to emerge from the shadows on the walls, tall and large warriors. These are the beings I read about as a girl, and now they are here before me.

The warriors surrounded Tepa and Aether. She did get a little nervous when they spoke, saying, "Now we have the key, so let us begin the recovery strategy for those who have been waiting patiently for years. It is time to bring forth the reckoning."

The time had come to return evil back to its dark hole in a dimension that could never be retrieved. Once the Great Aralia King and other alien leaders they were holding were released, they would close the entry forever.

Tepa listened to every word. They brought out emotions that she could not hide. She began to sweat. Her face was dripping sweat heavily. She could not control herself.

Her body began to change during this time. Tepa was in great pain and could not understand why this was happening to her. Her hair on her shoulders turned to gold and felt heavy but light as a golden see-through shield. Tepa's back was transforming into something that she could not see but felt. She thought, am I turning into something that is horrible for anyone to look at? She screamed inside, what am I to do?

After hours of transformation, the hull opened, and gold imaging mirrors embodied Tepa's figure. Tepa observed her new form and tried to speak out. When she did, her voice flowed with power that shattered the mirrors.

She thought, is this the destiny my family spoke of? If so, I do not desire it. She screamed inside, someone, please help me. Tepa believed the only one who helped her was Chief Amasis. She remembered that he always showed up when she needed help the most. Trying to control her voice, she asked for Chief Amasis but realized he could not be there. How could he still be alive? She was confused. Tepa thought, why and how could he be here? But she felt his presence.

Tepa heard voices of discussion about her, which got her attention away from her body pain. She moved toward them to interrupt their discussion. They were concerned about Tepa. She was the only factor and important to everything that had to take place.

She said again, in a voice she was trying to control, "What of Chief Amasis?"

A recognizable voice responded quietly, calling out to her, saying, "Tepa, it is me."

It was her grandfather. Tepa wanted to run to him but could not move. She was extremely glad to see him. She tried to tell him everything with a shaken voice. Her grandfather instructed her to wait until she finished healing.

He said, "I waited for you to come." Aether quickly responded, saying, "I wanted to get here faster but had to let Tepa figure out how to walk her destiny." He could only be with her to protect her until this day.

Tepa's grandfather took her by the hand and led her into another chamber. But he assured her first not to be afraid; once she finished, she would start the beginning of her true destiny. Grandfather encouraged her and said, "It is important to complete your transformation." Tepa told him that she would make it through it as long as he was with her.

In the chamber, Tepa's heart and body became strong and powerful. Tepa raised her hand, and the wrap around her wrist broke like a thread. She learned more vital information during the time spent in the chamber. Learning of other alien races and worlds. She received information and clearly understood.

In the chamber, tears rolled down her face; she felt something more happening to her that was changing her essence. Tepa got incredibly quiet, and her tears dissipated.

The chamber door opened. It was late in the night. Tepa walked out, and Aether waited at the opening. He said to Tepa, "Now let us see what you have learned."
She said, "There is no way you could begin to know what I have become. I could hurt you badly."
Aether walked away and called her "the birth of the prophecy gene."

Tepa gave him an incredibly surprised look when he allowed his body to change. Wings proceeded out and opened wide from his back. He grew taller than she knew. At that moment, she realized that everything was getting real.

Tepa learned in the chamber how to change her body and how to control her power. She opened her beautiful golden wings and grew larger than Aether. They both looked at each other and flew into the universe. They flew at a speed that no alien could really see them.

In the universe, there were many asteroids that gravitated at that speed. They were moving so fast a large asteroid was pulled into their pathway. Aether was far away from Tepa and saw that she was faced with an obstacle. He did not understand why she was not moving out of the way.

Aether panicked and aimed to get to her and remove her from the danger. Tepa went through the asteroid and appeared behind Aether. When Aether saw her, he was shaken a little. He had seen many things but never this type of strength and speed.

Aether remembered a story told years ago of a world of women with great strength.

In this world, there was a rare, beautiful princess whose partner was brought to her from a spiritual place where power was luminous and could not be touched.

This universe was closed to all. No one could survive the essence. She gave birth to a son who was stolen right after birth and taken to another universe. He was found much later as a young kid, who grew to be a great leader. His name was Chief Amasis. No doubt Aether knew that she was an ancestor of the planet of women, as he watched Tepa and the way her body moved as she flew through the universe, got his full attention.

Tepa was moving so fast that he lost sight of her. He returned to the hull and talked with Tepa's grandfather and the warriors. He told them Tepa had left the universe. Aether said he was not sure where she went or when she would return. He told them, "She is ready, and knowing her ancestors, they are waiting to engage her.

" Tepa changed after entering space among the stars and the universe, becoming someone great, strong, and moving with more power than a warrior.

Meanwhile, Aether and the other warriors realized they had to continue fighting in the hope that Tepa would come back soon. Tepa's grandfather was concerned about the role the key played in the legacy.

He questioned what his granddaughter had become and believed that Tepa would return for crucial answers so that she could go forward. He was searching all of the information on the genes of the key to stop the evil alien.

Tepa was reaching new capabilities, moving throughout, and seeing locations never seen before. Watching aliens, unlike her or her old self, enjoying the fact that no one can see her. The material that her wings and body were covered with was camouflage like the material Tepa found in the library, which now seemed so long ago.

Finally relaxed enough to remember others, Tepa felt honored to be with the warriors. The experience of power from the handprint on the box that she and Eaton touched, now after revealing her power and skills as a formidable fighter, she was beginning to accept these changes. While moving through the galaxy, she finally felt reassured by the transformations to her body.

Suddenly, Tepa stopped, and she realized she had no control. Her strong, magnificent wings wrapped around her body, creating a shape like a missile. Tepa's direction of travel changed; she could not stop herself from traveling at such a high speed, moving far from the worlds she knew. Then, instantaneously and completely, she stopped in space. Tepa heard a buzzing sound coming from her body, and then she heard a sound coming from the space in front of her.

Space opened directly in front of Tepa; she was taken back

while moving through the split into the universe. Tepa could not turn around because she had no control over her movement. She entered this amazing world; space closed behind her.

Everything around her was still and quiet. There were many worlds in her vision, different from her universe. There were two suns, one with electrical spheres coming out of it. The other was farther away, both creating light that illuminated an array of many colors. There were scents of fragrances in space, from plants and flowers throughout. Everything was large. She had never seen anything like this before.

Tepa did not know what to do next; she just stared out in limbo. The smells and lights relaxed her. Her body shell started to cover up with a mist. The mist activated change to her form by releasing her extremities.

The transformations continued altering the range of her vision. Her vision's clarity was more translucent, strengthening her ability to see differently than before and her extreme capability to see movement miles away.

As Tepa continued to focus, she saw large images. They came

closer, and her sight cleared to see magnificent figures right in front of her. Tepa was not shaken after facing the figures, which started to look familiar. She also knew that she was brought here for a reason. She believed they were a welcoming committee.

The closer the figures came, the more astonished she became. There was no fear, nor did Tepa feel out of place because of her transformation. Her recent look seemed common among the figures in this universe, but her image changed even more as she became taller.

The aliens looked like her, and they greeted and smiled with approval. Tepa felt and heard their thoughts and feelings. The aliens motioned her to follow them. After surrounding her, they took her to the heart of the city to the queen.

Queen Amasis, known throughout the dimensions, sat upon a throne made for the heavens. Strings of gold, gems, and diamonds fell around her. It was natural in this mysterious planet in space and this dimension of time.

The queen appeared out of concern when Tepa was transitioning. She intentionally watched her progress to finish successfully. She understood the importance of having success in the results that would affect many dimensions as they anxiously waited for her transition to complete and reveal assurance of the ancestorial interstellar plan.

Tepa was born with the genetic material in her genes from the queen's brother, Chief Amasis. Aliens appeared through dimensions to witness a birth predicted by the angels. Tepa's family saw aliens appear out of space. They were there to identify if she was born with the special gene and who would be the chosen alien spoken about many years ago. Tepa would be the key to the destruction of the evil aliens.

The young princess patiently waited after Queen Mother left to go to another dimension to ensure the legacy would be saved. Thousands of years passed, and time moved in slow motion. Until one day, the queen was awakened by the sound of a vigorous heartbeat. From that moment, she began to send messages to her brother, who found him in a vision of the Great Kings, and he was saved by warriors.

The queen had been connected to Tepa all her life; she knew

when she was in trouble. Hearing Tepa breathing and screaming, she knew that Tepa was in trouble, and the queen sent her thoughts. Chief Amasis appeared at the hospital where Tepa and her grandfather were staying.

When Tepa was being attacked, Chief Amasis quickly stepped in to save her and left as soon as he removed the evil alien from attacking her again. Tepa was still being led to the queen, who was preparing and ready to answer all of Tepa's questions.

A chamber was created for Tepa thousands of years before her birth, and this time, it was to help her through her transition. The chamber was full of pertinent information to protect her until she reached the entrance into the hidden universe. Although Tepa did not understand the meaning of her power, she would know everything soon.

Tepa arrived at a planet that was the largest located in the hidden universe. She was overwhelmed as she walked among the most perfect tall beings. They were different colors. Their bodies glowed like waterfalls. In front of her, she saw something that made her stop because it took her breath away. The waterfall looks like gold glistening and pouring down into a deep opening flowing out into the abyss.

As Tepa proceeded through the gold pathway, she saw it! A revealing image behind a waterfall to camouflage a huge stunning castle. When Tepa reached the front of the beautiful but intricate place, she saw her home within the building. The castle looked like the home of her ancestors but more advanced than the castle in Aralia.

Tepa walked in, feeling at ease and close to her true ancestors. The building was extremely large and constructed with a technology structure that was fully see- through.

Walking through the see-through castle, Tepa rose to a high elevation. She saw within dimensions. Her breath was taken away to full dizziness. Tepa entered the last ice stone doors, hearing an outwardly not just outwardly, but inwardly voice speaking about the passing of the years.

The beautiful, tranquil voice spoke of a tragedy that happened thousands of years ago, saying there was a time when other aliens were allowed to enter the hidden universe. "The aliens saw riches never seen before. Those not born in the hidden universe worshipped material things and the value of what they saw. They believed this universe had more than enough and decided to take from us.

"They were selfish aliens, and the hidden universe recognized their evilness. The aliens, not knowing the power in the hidden universe, made the worst decision and caused a change to take place. "The mistake was letting the aliens stay while knowing that they could not be trusted.

The aliens who lived in the hidden universe thought them to be harmless. They had not encountered these types of aliens before, where they worship riches. They underestimated their greed and did not know the suffering they would have from their greed.

"Word went out among the worlds. The queen went into a quiet place for childbirth. It was a place where only the queen would be. While the queen gave birth, one of the outside aliens came to find her. The aliens from outside the hidden universe started to steal valuables. All while most of the queen's guards were in reflection.

"There was plenty of excitement about the birth. It was a special birth because it would be a son. In this universe, there are many worlds and special planets, not like other universes. A world of powerful mystic female aliens called Planet Paradox. The birth was special because a son would be born, which only happens every thousand years.

"Something miraculous was happening in the hidden universe of the world of women. The alien son would be special and would mate with another from one of the other worlds from the hidden universe. This was written for this time. An act predicted that the two would create a bond of strength, power, and intelligence far beyond other aliens."

"The birth of the son came closer. The outside aliens found their way to the queen. As the birth began, they waited for the birth to be completed and then came into the queen's room to take her son. Sorrow went out into the universe because this was an important child.

The alien had a plan to use the queen's son to force the worlds to give them more riches. The thief made it out of the hidden universe and waited for the others who never came. The thief's actions caused dramatic deviations in the dimension.

"Word went out among the universes of the first-born son's kidnapping. The thief became frightened and left the child on a faraway planet. The child could not be found until, one day, the child found us. Now, on this day, we welcome our ancestor's family, who have the gene that will change the universe. We waited for a long time for you to find us."

Tepa entered an open, flawless, exquisite corridor with colors streaming through. A shade opened, and there she was, Queen Amasis. She was a figure of stunning power that flowed in her presence. The shades of colors gave off illuminations that streamed and joined Tepa's newly transformed body.

The queen stood in the presence of a prophecy, the gene that will make changes in universes, and she gazed at Tepa and said, "Tell me about your travels." She asked Tepa how long she had known that she had the gene spoken in prophecy thousands of years ago. She replied, "The reality of having been chosen to be a part of this important task was a part of my consciousness for a long time."

The queen conveyed her happiness from Tepa's successful transition, with magnitude differences in her genetic makeup, which stemmed from the queen's own brother.

At the time of Tepa's birth, her family witnessed angels appearing from space, sent to see if she possessed the special gene foretold prophecies spanning thousands of years. Tepa held the key to vanquishing the evil aliens, and her arrival was eagerly anticipated."

Queen Amasis believed she did not have a lot of time before Tepa had to leave for the battle, and she had to finish training with her. This training was vastly different from the warriors. Tepa replied, "Why? I have learned so much about fighting."

Queen Amasis told her it was not only about fighting; it was about the gift in her that would change the wars. Tepa understood that she needed to learn how to use her power and purpose. "Afterward, we can finally talk about how we will take care of evil aliens."

Chapter Eighteen

EATON AND THE KEY

After Tepa left with Aether to find her grandfather, Eaton started a journey to find his purpose. He was concerned about letting Tepa return to space alone. After watching out for her, the tribal aliens, and all the family quietly for years, it was a change for him. Tasked to protect Tepa, just as all of his ancestors did for her family, Eaton never knew why but felt it was the right thing to do. It became a more serious task when his father was taken. He began to remember the path he was on before his first Season of the Stars, which changed his life.

He lost his father during that time, and he believed he would have answers. They never found him. He left for the Season of the Stars and never returned. Eaton understood his destiny was important, and he felt the pull to step out of his comfort zone. He heard a quiet voice inside him calling.

Eaton returned to Tepa's grandfather's office looking for more information. A sister from the tribal community came to Eaton and handed him a book. He had never seen this alien before, and she swiftly disappeared after she gave it to him.

The book had a note attached to it, and it was from Aether. The note he received from Aether read, "Eaton, this is an important book. Read it now because we need you. Your destiny is here now. This book will reveal your family's legacy. We will be here waiting for you."

Eaton took the book with unbelievable excitement, saying, "I feel that if I open this book, it will change my life."
He opened it, hearing Aether's voice say, "Read it now because we need you." His heart was beating rapidly.

Searching for answers to take him back with Tepa and Aether, he still did not realize how his life was going to change. The book gave him instructions on getting into the room, which was already waiting for him. The book led him back to the library, a familiar place. The same place where the four stairways were located.

When Eaton walked in with the book, he noticed one of the staircases had an engraved sign that matched the top of the book. Eaton was curious and slightly confused about what was happening, so he walked into the staircase that moved him up the stairs to the corridor.

There, he found a room that was not like the staircase Tepa had followed. His staircase ended with a door to a large room. As the door opened, he saw a room with a large chamber inside. The chamber's color matched the book he was carrying.

Eaton started carefully walking with haste into the chamber. The book automatically lifted from his hand and magnetically placed itself into an open slot, and the door of the chamber closed behind him.

The book came alive in the chamber. Eaton was flooded with information quickly, and he received facts about his ancestors and learned about his birthright and destiny. He listened to everything, observing and searching through pictures that appeared all over the wall.

Eaton discovered hidden mysteries in the chamber, causing him to allow anxiety from sudden fear to assume him. He was near denial and thought maybe he should just walk away until he realized how this action would interfere with him seeing his family and Tepa again. He pulled himself together and listened to the book.

This book was written in an old language, one that Eaton's mother taught him. A language his father insisted he learn and said he would need one day. He lost his father during the Season of the Stars celebration and never knew the level of challenges his father endured.

Eaton learned his father was a powerful alien, a young aristocrat, who had the ability to move into time. He visited the time of the Great Kings, watched lights from the stars in the universe, and enjoyed the designs of drawing from gifted kings.

There was a king named Odonias who was admired by everyone in the galaxies. He had a special gift of good persuasion. King Odonias could move on the hearts of all aliens. His presence kept the peace and controlled evildoers from causing disaster.

"Certain Elder Kings did not like how one king was capable of persuading other kings to make decisions. The kings became jealous of King Odonias and decided to get rid of him. The kings got the help of the evil aliens from the dark hole. This was an act that would never be forgotten.

The evil aliens showed concern for the kings and gave them their word they would not kill King Odonias, just remove him. "They tricked him into participating in a race through an asteroid, and once he passed, they grabbed him and covered his face and mouth. They locked him in a dark place in the asteroid. He was never seen again.

"The universe changed. Evil aliens tricked the kings and caused more pain and sickness than ever. The kings never knew this could happen; they had remorse for what they had done to King Odonias and understood that he had kept evil away. The kings were taken away by the evil aliens and locked away in the black hole.

"The universe was altered because the special gift of persuasion was no longer around. The wars between good and evil began. King Odonias was lost and could not be found again. If you are reading this book, accept who you are and believe that you are part of a legacy that is needed to help the universe fight evil.

You are an ancestor of King Odonias. The king's father, Great King Odonias, placed a child on the planet where a missing child from the hidden universe was taken.

"The child was to grow up with the young boy named Amasis and watch out for him. The alien child was from King Odonias world. They both were lost after the battle of the evil alien taking the warriors' alien tribes to their planet.

Both of them were pulled onto a planet with other aliens, where no one knew who they were. The warriors learned much later that Chief Amasis was the missing alien from the hidden universe because of a sword the young child was carrying. Your ancestor was from King Odonias's home.

"King Odonias's father had already foreseen this would take place. In many years, there will be a young girl born with a gift in her genes from the hidden universe of Queen Mother

Amasis and a young boy born with a gift from King Odonias's world.

Who will be the key to ending evil?

Together, they will lead a war to release those who have been

taken to the black hole where evil lives.

"As you read, your gift is awakening in you. It is your time and

summoning. The time is now to remove the evil aliens born out of

hatred and jealousy created by the Elder Kings thousands of years

ago."

Eaton was receiving all kinds of information at one time as

he found himself in a chamber almost like the chamber Tepa was

in. As it revolved, lights, pictures, and even his great ancestor, King

Odonias, entered the chamber and taught him more about his gift

and how to use it.

Eaton felt himself changing. He thought his face was burned

really bad from the heat he thought he had experienced. Later, he

was able to see that it was an illusion. Eaton knew he had changed.

He could feel it in everything in him.

When the chamber opened, he walked out and saw everything from a distinct perspective. He heard many voices of aliens but focused on searching for Tepa. He knew he had to find her, for without her, he understood he was not able to complete the task asked of him.

Amid the multitude of alien voices echoing, Eaton's focus remained fixed on finding Tepa. He understood that without her, he could not fulfill the task set before him. But he wondered how Tepa, a seemingly ordinary girl, could be effective in the battle against the evil aliens residing within the black hole.

Tepa Returns

Tepa returned to the warriors, and not long after, Tepa, Aether, and the warriors were fighting. She noticed that her grandfather was exceptional as a fighter and warrior. Everyone, including the warriors, was excited about Tepa and her gifts.

As a team, they pushed the evil aliens through space. The fight continually advanced to the black hole where evil aliens lived. Tepa certainly never envisioned her destiny fighting in space. She had not missed a target; every move she made was as if she had her skills and gifts all her life. Tepa was optimistic and completed every action for her destiny to save the universe.

Tepa's grandfather never got a chance to share the entire plan with her. He wished he had the opportunity to have warned her about the strategy to overtake the black hole. Tepa moved fast, causing her to be farther ahead of everyone. Grandfather saw how she moved and quickly realized she already knew what was going to happen before it happened.

He waited on Tepa because he knew once they entered the black hole, the gate would open, and evil aliens would be there.

They needed to let the evil aliens take them hostage. Tepa sent her grandfather a message of telepathy. He heard her voice; she said just three words, "I know, Grandfather." He heard her, and it comforted him to know she had evolved into the true key, with full progression and maximum ability. He thought, these changes happened so quickly.

This was a dangerous setup for Tepa, but she knew this would be the only way evil aliens would think they could finally remove all good.

Once they captured Tepa, all other leaders left from the new generation would ensure they would never be controlled by the warriors again.

Tepa pushed through the gates with a team from the hidden universe. Her grandfather saw what she was expecting to see. Tepa learned a lot from the queen, who taught her how to see and listen. She learned the truth about her ancestors.

They were perfectly preserved in the dark hole, as leaders from generations and others, missing for almost a thousand years. Some had been missing for a hundred years, and some, later years.

Tepa gasped at the sight of her parents in a large cavity in space, surrounded by aliens and the animals from the Old World, ready to kill everyone if anyone tried to escape. Tepa, Aether, and her grandfather allowed themselves to be captured so they would be taken to the captives. The evil aliens threatened them and pushed them to join the others.

Following the plan to retrieve their tribes and kings, Grandfather commanded everyone to drop their weapons and enter the large cavity. As they were being loaded in a chamber located in the cavity, Tepa thought about Eaton, not knowing the changes in Eaton's life.

They were all put together, and the captives talked to the warriors and identified family connections, mostly all the tribes left in the valley by Chief Amasis, captured by the original inhabitants and the trained animals. Some turned evil, and some did not. Those who fought against evil were taken to the black hole to be placed with the other captives to stay until the reckoning.

Without the evil aliens knowing, the kings and other great leaders would not have been able to continue to use their gifts. Some of the kings were sent to find Chief Amasis because his sister, the queen, heard his concerns and knew he needed help. She sent them to him in a vision. The Great Kings were told the evil aliens had a plan to capture him.

They were coming for Chief Amasis because they realized he was the lost child from the hidden universe. They waited too late. They got there and saw he was not there. They took the alien tribes that were left before the fight of Moab.

After Chief Amasis left the valley to the plains and mountain, the dimensions opened in the valley, coming for Chief Amasis. The alien's goal was to get to the special alien leaders. The tribes were startled by memories of the stories told and how the leaders of the original evil alien race could move through dimensions to other universes. They never thought they would experience this happening to them. Evil aliens came from the dark hole to capture more warrior families, and they moved them through the dimensions to the evil aliens' chambers.

Tepa stood, looking like a great warrior princess. Showing respect for warriors, kings, chiefs, and leaders and seeing and believing in her destiny took her breath away. She remembered all the stories told to her by her grandfather.

Every word read to her was to bring her to this place. Tepa was so glad to know the truth. It did not take long to understand how they were still living; they were known to live thousands of years. They were all part of the universe and joined spiritually.

Although they were captured, she knew they could have left at any time, and they functioned freely and with control. They were waiting for something or someone to complete a task. Tepa told the leaders they were captured, but all was not lost, that they should not be disappointed.

The leaders replied, at the same time, that they already knew how things would end; they had been waiting for a long time, and it was worth the wait. The alien leaders told Tepa that she was not alone, and she did not let them down. This was the beginning of the end of evil in the universe.

Her grandfather called out to Tepa and said, "You are not alone because you are not the last of the gene of warrior kings who will free us."

Then she saw her parents. She thought with humiliation of how her body had changed, and they could not know who she had become. Her parents told Tepa that they were hoping for her arrival and knew she would survive her transition. They touched her and told her she was beautiful, that they were proud of her, and that they were glad to see her.

Tepa could not get her words out fast enough before she saw the one dressed as a king with something around his head stopping him from talking and speaking. Her parents said, "He was the young king. He has been waiting on you, Tepa!"

Aether told everyone to get prepared. It was time. He came to the leaders with warriors and told the leaders to follow him. The war between good and evil had begun; the warriors that followed them through the black hole were attacking evil aliens through dimensions.

Aether had the leaders follow him to the structures and thought he needed to secure everyone as the warriors focused on the battle with evil aliens. Aether, the captain of the warriors was tasked to bring Tepa to the hostages, and he had.

Chapter Nineteen

THE FAVOR OF GOD

The young king was quiet until he felt Eaton's presence inside of him. This let him know it was time to find the other key, Tepa. Who was out fighting with the warriors. Aether saw the changes in Tepa as she fought. Every hit created electrical power, and it practically burned the alien and anyone close to it to dust. She was relentless. She began to hear Eaton. He told her to be ready and said, "Tepa, I need you."

Tepa turned, thinking he was behind her, but she did not see him. She thought, it is all in my mind, or Eaton has changed and can talk to me by mind transference? The warrior was told to find Tepa and bring her to the hostages. She arrived with the warrior, to someone with their head covered.

As she approached the alien with the cover over him, the leaders looked concerned. Tepa asked, looking ready to conquer. Her face turned Aralia red, and her structure changed to protective reinforcement. She was thinking, what is wrong with everyone? She knew he was a king that she stood in front of, and he wrote a note and asked, "Tepa, have you heard from Eaton?"

She said out loud, "Eaton! How do you know Eaton?"

There was a man walking and directing the king he said, "I am Eaton's father, and this is his mother. We are the descendants of the Great Kings of Persuasion. There was a time when our alien race ruled the universe by persuasion of good."

Looking at Tepa with a look she recognized, he asked, "Have you heard from Eaton? Has he contacted you?" Tepa replied "Yes," and said, "I was thinking of him." Eaton's father asked again, "What did he say?" she replied to his father "He told me to be ready because he needs me."

The king reached for another piece of paper, his hands moving quickly, and wrote, "It is her; she is the one, the other key." Everyone but Tepa understood. The young king made his way to Tepa, touched her hand, and revealed himself. "Greetings, Tepa. I am King Odonias."

She knew him from the story her grandfather read to her, and about him and his queen, she quickly asked, "What can I do?" with great concern. Tepa said to King Odonias, "I have been with Queen, Odonias."

He said, "Did she trust you with an item?" King Odonias knew the queen would have sent what he needed to recover quickly. He asked Tepa, "Where is the special gift the queen gave you when you visited her?" Tepa said to him, "I do not have a special gift." But she remembered when the queen held her, she felt the queen placing something in her armor.

She quickly went into her armor and said, "She told me to always carry this with me wherever I go." Tepa removed a small round crystal box and said, "This might be what you are looking for."

It was a crystal blue shiny capsule in a box, placed on her, Tepa thought, to protect her. The queen knew she would see King Odonias. Then, King Odonias held out his hand, and Tepa placed the crystal in his hand.

When the crystal touched his hand, the entire chamber where all the hostages were living lit up. King Odonias's body lifted high in the air, and his power and Tepa's together blew the top off the chamber.

Suddenly, there was a loud noise from the top of the chamber, from the malevolent force that controlled the evil aliens throughout the universe and dimensions. Four special pursuit warriors tracked him to the dark hole. They were told not to fight him but to encourage him to wrath. What the warriors did barely affected the malevolent force. Its response to the warriors nearly wiped them out.

Tepa was preparing to fight him, not realizing that she

was the reason he was there.

Tepa rose up to see outside the chamber and saw the malevolent force. It spoke to her, saying, "Tepa, I have heard so much about you. I knew you before you were born. I was among those who witnessed your birth. Now, I demand your care, Tepa, and your power of goodness. If you let me in and join me, we can control all the dimensions and universes."

The malevolent force's voice was pulling at her spirit, trying to induce her. She remembered the story of King Trios. With her power, she could see through the smoke and saw the demon's body. It was a figure twisted and contorted, features marred by the influence of darkness and evil. Its skin was slick and had scars from all the wars against it. It had limbs so unnatural and elongated, moving around.

Tepa knew to get hit once by the body of the malevolent force; it would be hard to get up. She heard Eaton speaking again, and he asked, "Are you all, right? Do not fight him because he will trick you."

Tepa told Eaton, "You are right, I will wait for you to arrive. Just hurry."

Aether found Tepa and the king; he protected them from the evil aliens while they waited for Eaton. He wanted to be ready so they could all control the malevolent force, the demon. Eaton said, "Once we are all connected to King Odonias, we will not be stopped, for it is our destiny."

The king was standing and waiting for Tepa to move as he asked. He knew her power because she had the genes of his wife, the queen. Tepa moved toward him with the force that no one could stop; she flew into the air. The malevolent force could do nothing but watch. She was moving so fast that she met the king with an intense, powerful thrust. Her power exploded all around, and the king was standing with Eaton when all the smoke disappeared. His eyes glistened with power. Eaton had suddenly appeared.

Tepa and Aether looked at him. He had transformed; his body was built more muscular, which made him stronger than before, and his height was like that of the warriors and Aether.

Eaton wore royalty armor and carried a positive charge in the atmosphere. King Odonias took Eaton by the hand, and they both sent power from their eyes into the universe. The power changed the evil alien's thoughts of evil. If they could not live for good, they would disintegrate in the galaxy, never to exist again.

The hostages were all freed, and the warriors began to transport them to the Aralia mountains. As they all began to celebrate the seasons of the stars, the Realms opened with a great force from the universe. The leader of the evil aliens did not change and was back.

King Odonias, Eaton, Tepa, Aether, warriors, and the leaders all came out into the universe. They were all ready to fight this evil demon, knowing that the power greater than all power would help them. The evil spirit was laughing, saying this time, he would make everyone his followers.

They fought with vigor, not giving up yet preparing to die if necessary before they allowed the tribal aliens to become evil.

But suddenly, the universe opened like a scroll, and the most beautiful place ever seen or imagined showed behind the great force. The universe was filled with a feeling of power, peace, and love.

Within this great force, a voice echoed and called out to the universe, saying to the malevolent force, "You have had your time, and you have lost." The mighty force was felt and heard all over the universe saying, "Go and never return." The power of his word was so strong it struck the malevolent force and destroyed it. The mass turned into a vaporous powder.

Then the voice said, "Job well done to everyone." This powerful, beautiful, loving spirit began calling all the ancestors by name, saying, "The time has come. Others are waiting for you. It has been, for some, thousands, and others, hundreds of years. It is time for the new generation to lead the universe."

Tepa was very emotional. She felt the loss of their ancestors, who could have taught her more about who she had become. She wanted to scream loudly but did not because she knew her voice had great power. Then, seeing her parents and grandfather, she realized everything would be fine. Seeing her friends also made her realize that she was not the only one losing her ancestors.

Eaton and Aether also lost family ancestors. They all knew that one day, they would see their ancestors again. They all continued their mission to embrace the teaching of **'Goodness is in the Midst of Power'** to the tribal planets, which was an honorable act. As the alien's heart grew strong from the energy received from the effect of goodness, the universe became strong amid the midst of power from goodness. There was love between Tepa and Eaton, understanding how important the gifts they were given and the reason they were given to them.

They would go out and learn more about themselves before the universe found out about them. One day, if ever faced again with evil, they would be ready. They both went out into the universe to explore.

Aether was tasked to build up the strongest military, teaching the warriors' way of defense to the communities and enhancing their fighting abilities.

The elders were back among their tribal race, planning strategy for the future of Aralia and other planets. Tepa, Eaton, and Aether were the new leaders of the universe and would be known as the powers of good to the summit of the planets and to other worlds in the galaxies throughout the universe.

Conclusion:

As they ventured forth, their fame spread like cosmic ripples of tales and exploits that reached the farthest corners of the universe. They became known by their titles:

Eaton the Persuader, of the universe. Tepa, the infamous great princess, the Power Ball, the one who dominated physical and electrical power. Aether, the leader of the angelic warriors.

The leaders gave each of them approval to represent on their own as ambassadors for the leaders, to carry the message of:

GOODNESS IS IN THE MIDST OF POWER

Teaching the universe that true strength resided not just in raw power but in the virtuous intentions behind it.

They embodied the perfect balance of power and benevolence, and they were a testament to what unity and goodness could achieve.

Their journey continued, for the universe was vast, and there were still challenges to face and worlds to explore. As the heroes set forth, the universe awaited their next chapter, knowing that their destinies were forever intertwined with the fate of the cosmos.

They strode with courage, united by love, purpose, and a shared commitment to protecting the universe from darkness. Their legacy would endure, and their names would be whispered among the stars for eternity. For in the grand tapestry of the cosmos, they were the shining beacons of hope, the guardians of goodness, and the living testament to the *"Favor of God."*

The journey continues...

ABOUT THE AUTHOR

As a child, I grew up in a busy household with many siblings. I used to find quiet corners where I could let my imagination run wild creating stories. My mother, my eternal muse, fueled my creativity until her passing. Life after that took a turn as I was thrown into the role of a caretaker, leaving no time for my imagination.

Fast forward through the years I earned my bachelor's degree in business and began my journey in corporate America. During the next 30 years I experience great success, climbing the corporate ladder in the tech world as a project manager, while being married and raising a family.

During retirement, I found my love for writing came back. Transitioning into the realm of literature, I embarked on a journey as a novelist. Crafting tales that transcend reality's confines to explore the intricate tapestry of human existence.

Within the pages of my first published novel, Planet Aralia, Journey among the stars. Readers are transported to worlds shape by technology. Where the complexities of human emotion intertwine with the ever- evolving landscape of progress. With meticulous attention to detail and a knack for character development. I weave protagonists who mirror the resilience and grace.

Through my novels, I aspire not only to entertain but to inspire. Leaving readers captivated by the boundless power of imagination and the indomitable spirit of humanity. With each turn of the page, I invite them into a realm where dreams take fight and stories breathe, guided by my unwavering dedication to crafting narratives that linger long after the final chapter.